SANTA
GOT RUN OVER BY A
VAMPIRE

NEW ORLEANS

NOCTURNES

CARRIE PULKINEN

This is a work of fiction. Names, characters, places, and incidents are either the product of the author's imagination or are used fictitiously, and any resemblance to actual persons living or dead, business establishments, events, or locales, is entirely coincidental.

Santa Got Run Over by a Vampire

Contact Information: www.CarriePulkinen.com

Cover Art by Rebecca Poole of Dreams2Media
Edited by Krista Venero of Mountains Wanted

First Edition, 2020
ISBN: 978-1-7347624-4-0

Father Christmas has just been damned to darkness.

Jane Devereux is adjusting to her new life as a nocturne fabulously. She runs the most popular nightclub in the French Quarter and is married to the hottest vampire in New Orleans.

When she accidentally runs over Santa Claus and has to turn him into a vampire to save him, her perfect undead life begins to crumble like a week-old sugar cookie.

Whoops.

Jane has three days to teach Santa the ways of the vampire and send him back to the North Pole in time for Christmas Eve.

Oh, and if that's not stressful enough, her dad is coming for Christmas.

And he doesn't know she's a vampire.

Or that she's married.

Double whoops.

Grab a mug of miracle cure and join the vamps of New Orleans Nocturnes in this fast, fun holiday read.

CHAPTER ONE

"You killed Santa." Gaston's mouth fell open as he stared at the strange man lying in the dirt.

"No." Jane shook her head and slammed the car door shut before creeping toward the body. City Park was eerily quiet, not a soul in sight to witness the whoopsie she'd just committed—yet another benefit of existing under the cover of night. Who said vampires were damned?

"I killed *someone*, yeah. But Santa isn't real." She toed the man's shoulder with her boot, but he didn't move.

Sure, he had white hair and a beard; he was a big guy, and hell, he looked like he might have been a jolly dude, but Santa? C'mon. It was a week before Christmas. What the hell would Santa Claus be doing in New Orleans?

Anyway, Santa was nothing more than a ploy made up by parents to finally get their kids to behave for at least a month out of the year. Jane knew this because it was the only thing that worked on her when she was little. Tell a six-year-old Santa wouldn't bring her a pony, and she'd eat her damn broccoli. Brussels sprouts too.

Gaston gently shut the passenger door of Genevieve,

his beloved Maserati Quattroporte, and ran his hand over the dent in the hood. "I forget just how young you are, *ma chère*. Santa Claus is most definitely real. I've known him since I was a wee tot."

Jane scoffed. This had to be the tallest of tall tales she'd ever heard from the ancient vampire. It was just like Gaston to blow off a possible manslaughter charge with a joke. "Right. You know Santa, and I'm the Easter Bunny."

"The Easter Bunny is a fae who chooses to take the form of a rabbit to honor Eostre, the goddess of spring. Santa assumes a human form."

She gaped at Gaston, trying to decide if he was yanking her chain, but he looked as serious as could be. He wore his dark hair pulled back in a band at the nape of his neck, and his ice blue eyes were calculating, cutting between the dead man and Jane. The muscles in his jaw were tense, which meant he was grinding his teeth, which meant, for like the third time since she'd met the man, he was actually concerned about a situation.

In fact, he hadn't said a word about the damage she'd done to Genevieve, and he loved that car more than he loved Cuervo-tainted O-negative.

Well, shit. "You're not kidding, are you?"

"I never kid about the fae."

She looked at the dead guy, tilting her head as the reality sank in. "Oh. My. Goat cheese pizza. I killed Santa." *And holy crap! Santa is real!*

Well, Santa *was* real…until she ran him over. She had so many questions, but she put a pin in it. Right now, they had a body to dispose of. Jane Devereaux would *not* be charged with murder.

"Wait. Santa is a fae? Aren't they immortal?"

Gaston's brow furrowed. "Every being has a weakness. Much like a stake to the heart can kill a vampire, it appears being run over by a sports car will be the end of this fae."

The man groaned, and a strange bubbling sound emanated from his throat. Jane's pulse sprinted as she knelt by his side. "Did you hear that, Gaston? He's not dead! I'm not the girl who single-handedly destroyed the nation's most precious holiday!"

This was just her luck, wasn't it? She'd begged Gaston for months to let her drive his Maserati—Ethan got to drive it, so why not her?—and he'd finally given in. But the first time she got behind the wheel, she lost control and plowed into the park, running over Santa Claus, of all people.

Gaston stood behind her so she had to crane her neck to look at him. Clasping his hands behind his back, he shook his head and made a *tsking* sound. "Asher will be along any minute now. You've got to turn him before the reaper arrives."

Turn him? *Oh, hell no.* "Not so fast, Lestat. He might live." And she was *not* sinking her fangs into Santa's neck. The dial on her moral compass might have shifted a bit since she became a vampire, but to turn the man who brought joy to millions of children around the world into a creature of the night? That sounded like the makings of a horror movie.

"Use your senses, young one," he snapped. "You can feel his imminent death if you'll focus for a devil damned minute."

"Hey, I just found out Santa Claus is real and that I almost killed him. Cut me some slack, old man." She rested a hand on Santa's chest. He was breathing...but barely. "And how can I *feel* his death coming on? I'm not a necromancer."

Gaston rolled his eyes. "Before the Supernatural World Order came into power and created our laws, vampires killed their victims. We drained them to the cusp of death, stopping just before the heart ceased to beat. Sensing that cusp is an innate part of you. An instinct. I can feel it from here. Focus, Jane, for once in your undead life."

She bared her fangs and hissed at the old-as-dirt vampire, but he didn't even flinch. "Fine. I'll focus. But you don't have to be such a Meanie McMeanie Pants about it. It's not like I did this on purpose." Why did it feel like she'd just been assigned Tim Allen's role in a darker version of *The Santa Clause*? Whatever happened, she was sure as shit not putting on this guy's coat.

Pressing her lips together, she stared at the fae's waning green aura and relaxed her mind. The moment she stopped her thoughts, her body recoiled. Sure enough, her instinct told her this guy wasn't just caroling at Death's door; he'd picked the lock and was about to step inside.

"What are we gonna do? We can't let Santa die." She rose to her feet and dusted the dirt from her jeans. "Oh, I know! We can call the necromancer, Jasmine. Once he passes, she can grab his soul and shove it back inside his body. He'll at least last long enough to do his thing on Christmas Eve, right? Then the elves can elect a new Santa."

"A zombie cannot perform his duties, and the fae cannot *elect* a new Santa. You must turn him, or there will be hell to pay."

She chewed her bottom lip and stared at her victim. "I don't want to be the gal who ruins the holiday, but I can't sire Santa Claus. He's all light and joy. I can't turn him into a nightmare before Christmas."

"Ruins the holi—?" Gaston looked at her like she had a second set of fangs growing from her gums. "Christmas will be the least of our worries. This man is the ruler of all fae. Their king. If you don't turn him, not only will you be charged with murder before the SWO—and staked, I might add—but you'll start a war between the fae and the vampires."

He clutched her shoulders and turned her toward Santa. "Now, get down there and make him undead before he's really dead."

Satan's balls. "Why does every little mistake a supe makes become the harbinger for war?"

Gaston crossed his arms. "This mistake was not little, but you can remedy it."

"But if I turn him, he'll be a vampire, not a fae. Will they even still accept him?"

"He'll be a hybrid, which is better than dead. We'll deal with the ramifications once his transformation is complete, but you are running out of time. Turn him now, Jane."

She fisted her trembling hands and gazed at the mess she'd made. Leave it to Jane Devereaux to find out Santa is real, and he's the ruler of the fae, *and* then kill him all in the same night. "I can't be his sire. He's way too important, and I'm a newbie vampire. You should do it. You've sired people before, so you know what you're doing."

"I'm not the one who ran him over. This is your problem, *ma chère.* You must take responsibility for your actions."

She growled low in her throat and kneeled next to the dying St. Nick. "If Ethan were here, he'd do it."

"I'd expect nothing less from him; he's your husband. I am not."

"But you're my grandpa, right? Kinda. That's got to count for something."

"I sired your sire. If I am your grandfather, that would make Ethan your father. Are you sure you want to tread down that path?"

"Ew. Yeah, that's a kink I could never get into. Let's not go there." Though vampires didn't actually need oxygen, she sucked in a deep breath to steel herself. "Okay, I can do this. Today will go down in history as the day Jane Devereaux saved Christmas."

"After she nearly ruined it."

"Whatever." She leaned down and bit into Santa's neck.

"Absorb his essence as you drink," Gaston said, "and use your magic to form a connection with him."

She only managed two sips of blood, and she hoped to Hades that was enough because damn… "Ack. He tastes like saltwater taffy, peppermint, and Coke Zero, with an extra heaping of high fructose corn syrup."

"He is a sugar fae, so that makes sense. Their entire diet consists only of sweets. Did you feel the connection form?"

She wiped her mouth with the back of her hand and scraped her tongue across her top teeth, trying to get rid of the saccharine flavor. "I think so."

"Good. Now, bite your wrist and get your blood into his mouth. Quickly. You're running out of time."

She sank her fangs into her arm and squeezed with her other hand. Vampire blood was as gooey as molasses, so she had to force herself to bleed. Once a thick drop pooled on her skin, she pressed her wrist to Santa's mouth. He didn't respond.

"He's not drinking." She rubbed her wrist over his lips, staining his pristine white mustache and beard. *Oops.*

"Give it time." Gaston loomed behind her, his tension rolling off him in waves, which made Jane even more nervous about what she was doing...damning Father Fucking Christmas to darkness. *Satan's balls on a silver platter!* She was in way over her head now.

Santa's bloodshot eyes flew open, and he latched onto her wrist, sucking like a Hoover on overdrive. *Ouch!*

"That's enough," Gaston said. "He'll drain you if you allow it."

Jane pried her arm away, and Santa's wounds healed in seconds. He sat up, rubbing his head until his gaze locked on her.

"Ho, ho, hello. What do you want for Christmas, young lady?" He held up a finger before she could answer. "Wait. Don't tell me. Jane Devereaux, your Christmas wish is to have your father accept you for who you are. That's not a gift I can give, I'm afraid. How about a pony instead?"

Jane's eyes widened, her mouth falling slack as Santa stiffened and fell backward into the dirt. "What the...? How did he...?" She was speechless, and Jane Devereaux was *never* speechless.

Her dad was coming to New Orleans for Christmas. It would be the first time he'd visited her new home. The first time he would meet Ethan. It would also be the first time she told him she was a vampire...and that she was married.

And Santa knew. *Holy Christmas cookies.*

Gaston paced toward Santa's head and slid his arms

beneath his shoulders. "Grab his feet. We'll put him in the backseat and take him home. The death sleep will keep him under until sunset tomorrow."

"I…" Jane blinked and scrambled to her feet to help Gaston get her new charge into the car. Though he was as bulky as a grizzly bear, their vampire strength made lifting him a breeze. Actually getting him into the backseat was another story.

Jane climbed in first, dragging him by the boots—which were not fur-lined like she'd expected. One of them came off in her hands, revealing a green sock with an image of whom she hoped was Mrs. Claus wearing a red corset and thong, posed like a pin-up girl.

He wore jeans and a blue flannel shirt with motorcycle boots and a leather jacket. As she took in his outfit, she realized his pants were undone, only half his shirt tucked in the front.

Why was Santa Claus standing by a tree near the edge of City Park, anyway? Surely he wasn't… She lifted the untucked edge of his flannel and dropped it like it was made of pure hellfire.

"Oh, man. He was taking a piss against the tree when I hit him." She just *had* to look, didn't she? Now she'd seen Santa's Yule log, and *that* was a sight she could not unsee, no matter how badly she wanted to. "This is *so* not how I imagined Father Christmas."

"He's off-duty." Gaston shoved him the rest of the way in and closed the door, banging it against his head.

"Good thing he's unconscious." She slipped his boot back on his foot and moved to climb into the front seat. He could deal with his own zipper when he woke up. She wasn't getting anywhere near his candy cane.

"Oh, no, *ma chère*." Gaston wagged a finger at her. "You're not riding with me."

"You can't expect me to trek home in these heels." Jane gestured to her stilettos. "These boots were not made for walking."

He laughed. "You're not walking. You're riding." He jerked his head toward a big black Harley Davidson parked near the spot where Santa had lain.

"What in hell's name? That wasn't there before." She crept toward the bike, and it rolled backward, almost as if it were shy. It had a wide leather seat and a black satin finish on the engine parts. Not too flashy, but the sucker looked faster than a vampire on his way to an all-you-can-drink blood buffet. "Is it a magical motorcycle or something?"

"Or something. I'll drive Genevieve. You ride Blitzen home."

"He named his bike after a reindeer?" She glanced at the side of the gas tank, and sure enough, the name Blitzen was scrawled across it in bright red paint. "There's a problem with your plan, man. I don't know how to ride a motorcycle." And it wasn't something she could learn in fifteen minutes, especially when this machine seemed almost...alive.

Gaston arched a brow. "You can ride a horse, can you not?"

"Well, duh. I am a Texas girl. Raised on a ranch before my dad became governor."

"Blitzen should be no different." He opened the driver's side door.

"I've got news for you, Louie. Motorcycles and horses are not the same. You may need to find your meals somewhere other than Bourbon Street for a while. I think the alcohol is affecting your brain."

"Sadly, I'm way too sober at the moment, and I'm surprised you can't see through the glamour. Try touching it."

"Touching the motorcycle?"

"Touching Blitzen."

"Okay." She reached a hand toward the bike and stroked the handlebar. But it didn't feel like cool steel. Instead, it was warm and...was that fur?

She blinked, and the magic cloaking Blitzen slipped away, revealing an honest-to-goat-cheese reindeer. Antlers and everything! "Whoa."

Blitzen blew a puff of breath through his nose and stamped his hoof, looking none too happy that she'd just flattened his owner.

"Hey, boy." She rubbed his velvety nose. "I'm sorry about hitting Santa. He's going to be okay, though." *I hope.* "You wanna come home with us, and we'll get you something to eat?"

The reindeer grunted, which Jane took as a yes, so she texted Ethan: *Meet us at Gaston's and bring carrots. Lots of carrots.*

He replied with a thumbs-up emoji, and she grinned. Her husband had learned long ago not to question her weirdness, but, boy, did she have some explaining to do. To Ethan, and then to the Magistrate tomorrow night. Wouldn't that be a hoot and a half? Or possibly a death sentence, but she wouldn't worry about that right now.

She was about to ride a freaking reindeer!

CHAPTER TWO

"Giddy up!" Jane clicked her heels into Blitzen's sides, and he took off at a canter through the park. He didn't have a mane for her to hold on to like a horse would —which made steering a bitch—so she sank her fingers into his thick fur and held on for *deer* life.

Massive oak trees created a canopy over the narrow road winding through the park, and Jane grinned as she and Blitzen made their way toward Carrollton Avenue to head to Gaston's Garden District mansion.

Nobody blinked an eye as she rode a reindeer through Mid-City and hung a left on Washington Avenue. Not that there were all that many people out at three in the morning, but the few cars that did pass saw a tall brunette on a Harley, and Jane could live with that. She was already a vampire with a black belt in karate, but there was always room for improvement in the badassery department.

So she looked like a kickass biker chick, while she felt as giddy as a...well, as giddy as a kid on Christmas.

The traffic light turned red, and she was tempted to blow through it. But the low hum of an engine approaching sounded from behind her, and she glanced over her shoulder to glimpse a pair of headlights heading her direction.

With the way her luck had been running tonight, it would be a cop, and she wasn't in the mood to talk herself out of a ticket. "Whoa, boy." She tightened her grip on Blitzen's fur, pulling his neck back slightly like she would have done with reins or a horse's mane since she was riding bareback. The reindeer responded, slowing to a walk and then stopping on the white line before the crosswalk.

A bright blue Mustang pulled up beside them, and the driver lowered his window, letting out a low whistle. "What kind of horsepower does that thing have?"

Blitzen snorted, which must have sounded like she was revving her engine—thanks to the glamour—because Mr. Hotrod grinned and revved his in return.

Oh, he wanted a race, did he?

If Santa's reindeer could fly him around the entire world in one night, surely Blitzen could outrun a Mustang.

Jane flashed her most innocent smile and batted her lashes before arching a brow. "More than you can handle."

"Oh, you're on." He gripped the steering wheel and narrowed his eyes at the light.

Jane stroked Blitzen's neck and leaned forward to whisper in his ear, "Let's show him what you've got."

The light turned green, and in a flash of magic, Blitzen took off down the road at warp speed. Seriously, the scenery around her blurred into nothing, and if she hadn't been holding on, she'd have landed flat on her ass in the middle of the street.

Her eyes watered, and her lips parted, the speed making her mouth fill with air until her cheeks puffed like a blowfish and flapped in the wind. Drool trailed from the corners of her mouth to her earlobes, and just as she gained enough control to sit completely upright again, they arrived in Gaston's driveway.

His house was a two-story Victorian mansion, painted dark purple with white gingerbread trim. A rounded section in the front extended upward, above the second story, making it look like a castle tower. The perfect home for a vampire.

Jane blinked, wiping the tears and spit from the sides of her face. It took a moment or two for the shock to subside, and then she let out a maniacal giggle. Her jaw finally unlocked, so she closed her gaping mouth and grinned as she patted Blitzen's side.

"Yee haw!" she shouted. "That was amazing! How did you know where we were headed, boy?"

Gaston leaned against the hood of his car with his arms crossed. "He's Santa's reindeer. He always knows where he's going."

She slid off Blitzen's back, clutching his fur until her wobbly legs could hold her steady. *Man, what a rush!* "I've gotta get myself one of these."

"Put him in the back yard and then help me carry your fledgling inside."

Jane opened the gate and gave Blitzen a pat on his backside. "Go on, boy. I'll bring you some carrots as soon as Ethan gets here."

Blitzen nuzzled her cheek—his nose felt like warm velvet—and did as he was told, trotting into the back yard before Jane closed the gate. He was so much better than a pony.

"Grab his feet." Gaston pulled Santa out of the car by

his shoulders, and Jane caught his boots, being extra careful to steer clear of his midsection this time.

"Is this how you and Ethan got me home after I was turned?" With a boot under each arm, she helped Gaston get the unconscious vampire/ruler of the fae/giver of gifts up the front steps and into the living room.

"You were much easier to carry. Ethan cradled you in his arms and hissed if I got anywhere near you."

Her heart warmed as an image of Ethan carrying her into his house formed in her mind. Of course, at the time he thought she was his late fiancée reincarnated—which she wasn't. But that was okay. It all worked out in the end, and that was what mattered.

They laid Santa on the couch, and Gaston strode into the kitchen, taking a bottle of blood from the fridge and popping it in the microwave. "Tequila or rum?" he asked.

"I'll just take the blood, thanks."

He arched a brow. "You're now the sire to the ruler of the entire fae world."

Hell's bells. She plopped onto the loveseat and leaned her head back. What had she gotten herself into? "Got any whiskey?"

Gaston opened the cupboard to reveal a smorgasbord of liquor bottles.

"Make it strong, please."

When the microwave beeped, he poured the warmed blood into glasses and mixed the whiskey into both before settling on the cushion beside her. "I've been in plenty of jellies in my life, my friend, but this one takes the pie."

She took a giant gulp of her whiskey blood. "I think you mean 'jams' and 'cake,' but yeah. How am I going to talk my way out of this one? Who do I even need to talk to? The Magistrate? The SWO? Santa's wife?" She shuddered at the thought of *that* conversation. *Hello, Mrs. Claus. I almost killed your husband, but don't worry! I damned him to darkness instead.* Yeah…that would go over really well.

"One step at a time, *ma chère*. First, you'll get him registered and deal with the Magistrate. You're lucky you and he are friends. Vampires have been staked for far pettier crimes than this."

"Since when is adding to the vampire population a crime?"

Gaston sipped his drink, watching her over the rim of the glass like he expected her to answer her own question. "Have you forgotten the hell they gave Ethan when he turned you? And you were merely the *daughter* of someone important."

"Well, I…" She clamped her mouth shut. The wannabe Volturi Vampire Council had threatened to stake Ethan for not filing the proper paperwork before turning the Texas governor's daughter, but Jane had talked them out of it.

"I am not…" She was about to debate her own importance—Jane Devereaux wasn't *merely* anything—but her sexy-as-sin husband walked through the door, and she forgot all about the petty argument she was about to have.

Ethan wore jeans and a dark green t-shirt that made his emerald eyes pop. His wavy chestnut hair fell perfectly into place, and he smiled as his gaze met hers. "I brought the carrots." He held up three bags. "Is this enough?"

Jane rose to her feet and moved toward him. "Get over here, you scrumptious creature of darkness." She stepped into his arms and planted a ginormous kiss on his lips. She might have been in the biggest mess of her undead life, but she couldn't resist the hottest vampire in New Orleans. *Don't judge.*

An *mmm* sound resonated from his throat as he pulled her closer. "Now look what you've done. Vlad's awake."

She grinned at his use of her nickname for his dick, but the mention of dicks reminded her of another piece of meat she'd accidentally witnessed earlier tonight. "When you see the mess I've made, you'll want to impale me with a stake, not Vlad."

He gave her a quizzical look. "Does this have anything to do with the carrots?"

"Come see." She took his hand and led him around the sofa to see the sleeping Santa.

Ethan stopped, tilting his head and blinking at the man on the couch before cutting his gaze between Jane and Gaston. "Jingle my balls, is that who I think it is?"

"Your wife has gotten herself into a preserved cucumber, which means both you, as her sire, and I, as her accomplice, are marinating in the brine as well."

"You mean a pickle." Ethan looked at the bags of carrots in his hand. "Why do I have a feeling there's a reindeer involved?"

"Blitzen is in the backyard," she said.

"And Santa is here because...?"

Jane swallowed hard. "So, you know how you had to work on the end-of-year audit at the club tonight?"

"Yes, Jane. I do remember what I was doing half an hour ago." He set the carrots on the coffee table and pressed his lips into a thin line.

"Well, Gaston and I had just finished hunting for dinner, and I might have maybe convinced him to let me drive Genevieve."

Ethan glanced at Santa. "Okay..."

He knew. She could tell by the look on his face and the perturbed tone of his voice he knew exactly what happened, but he was going to make her say it.

Jane lifted her hands and dropped them at her sides. "You know how powerful that car is and how heavy my foot can be. I lost control and ran over Santa, and he was about to die so I turned him." She covered her face. "I turned Santa into a vampire."

Gaston lifted a finger. "A hybrid. Only a human can become a full vampire."

Ethan blinked rapidly, shaking his head like the blinking guy meme people use when they can't believe something. He looked just like that for a good thirty seconds before he finally spoke. "But…your dad will be here in three days."

"I know, I know. But Gaston said if I let him die, I'd be staked and start a war. Having Vampire Santa in the house for a few days will be better than fighting off the fae in front of my father."

"Jane." He took her by the arms. "The Council might still vote to stake you. A war might still happen."

"Okay, but a war *definitely* would have started if I didn't turn him. Now we have a chance it won't. And do you really think the Council would stake Jane Devereaux? After everything we've been through and talked our way out of?"

"She has a point, old friend. Turning him really was her only option." Gaston took Jane's unfinished glass of whiskey blood from the coffee table and downed the contents in one gulp.

Ethan blew out a heavy breath through his nose, gave Santa a hard look, and then softened his gaze at Jane. "I guess we'll be visiting the Magistrate tomorrow night."

Jane nodded. "You're not mad at me, are you?

He chuckled. "I could never be mad at you, princess."

She kissed his cheek. How the hell did she get so lucky? Well, lucky in love. In life, not so much at the moment. "I'll fix this. I promise."

"I know you will." Ethan grinned. "Is there really a reindeer in the backyard?"

"Yep. I rode him here."

His mouth dropped open. "You rode a reindeer?"

"He's faster than lightning too. Come say hi to Blitzen." She took his hand, grabbed the carrots, and led him down the hall to the back door while Gaston went to the kitchen for a refill.

"Wow." Ethan's eyes widened in wonder as they stepped onto the porch and Blitzen loped toward them.

Jane set the bags on the patio table and opened one before placing a carrot in Ethan's hand. "See if he's hungry."

He held out his hand, and Blitzen took the carrot between his teeth, pulling the entire thing from Ethan's grip before the reindeer lifted his head and let it fall into his mouth. When he finished chewing, he nudged Ethan's arm, asking for more.

Jane stood next to Blitzen and ran her palm over his side. "Question. Well, two questions, actually."

Ethan's smile brightened his eyes. "Shoot."

"Why can I say 'Christmas' out loud, when vampires were smote...smoted? Smited? Anyway, I can't say the first half of the word alone without feeling like I'm going to hack up a lung, but I can sing 'We Wish You a Merry Christmas' all day long."

"It's only the religious icon and his son's name vampires can't speak aloud. Christmas was built on pagan traditions, and the holiday has become so commercialized, it doesn't count."

Jane pursed her lips, nodding as she considered his explanation. "Gotcha. That makes sense, so on to question two. Since Santa is real, why is it that the parents buy all the presents for their kids, and adults don't even know he exists? What does he do if he doesn't deliver gifts?"

"He does deliver gifts," Ethan said, "just not to human kids."

"Why not?"

"Hundreds of years ago, he did. But once people stopped believing in magic, it got harder and harder for him to do his job. People didn't like the idea of a strange man sneaking into their homes at night, even if he was leaving presents behind."

"I can see how that would be creepy."

Ethan fed Blitzen another carrot. "So, he gave up on humans, and now he only brings presents to supe kids. He still embodies the spirit of Christmas—or Yule or Saturnalia, if you want to call it by its older names—and his magic is responsible for the holiday cheer, so I'm glad you decided to turn him. Who knows what would have happened to Christmas if you didn't."

"Gaston said he's known Santa since he was a kid. Didn't he start out human like you and me?"

"I certainly did." Gaston stepped onto the porch and sank into a chair before taking a sip of blood from his glass. "But a pack of shifters lived next door. My family was poor, so the wolves took me in and allowed me to celebrate the holiday with them. That's how I met Santa as a human."

Jane joined him at the table. "If you were practically raised by wolves, why are you a vampire now?"

Gaston chuckled and shook his head. "Daylight is approaching. You can sleep in the guest room until your charge awakens." He rose and sauntered inside, and Jane glared at his back. One of these days, Gaston would share his story. She'd make it her mission to get it out of him.

She and Ethan followed him inside, and as soon as she closed the back door, Gaston flipped a switch on the wall, activating his vampire protection system. Thick black shades descended over all the windows, and steel plates rose from the floors to block the doors. Nothing was getting in or out of Gaston's mansion until sunset...not even light.

CHAPTER THREE

When a "Ho, ho, ho" roused Jane from the death sleep, she rolled over, snuggling into her pillow and smiling. Instead of sugarplums, visions of her spicy-hot husband danced through her head, and she reached for him.

But the bed was empty.

"Ethan?" She rose onto her elbow and blinked the room into focus as another "Ho, ho, ho" sounded from the living room. "Hell's bells and buckets of eggnog, it wasn't a dream. Damn."

With a groan, she rolled out of bed and put on her clothes. She left her stilettos behind and padded barefoot down the stairs toward the sound. Gaston lounged in a recliner, reading from a thick volume of Edgar Allen Poe stories, and Ethan sat on the loveseat, his hands fisted on his knees, the tendons in his neck stretched tight as he ground his teeth. *Uh oh.*

"Hey, sweetheart." She sank down next to him, resting a hand on his thigh. "I see our new friend is up early."

"He's been *ho, ho, ho-ing* for an hour straight." His fists clenched tighter.

"Really?"

Gaston set his book on an end table. "He seems…how should I put this? Not quite right in the head. Did you notice any bleeding from his ears before you turned him?"

"No. Wait…are you saying I gave Santa brain damage?"

"Something is damaged," Ethan grumbled. "We need to get him to the Magistrate so he can get a feeding permit, but he's not interacting with us." He looked at her. "He needs his sire to explain what happened, but you've been sleeping."

Her nostrils flared as she huffed. It wasn't her fault the death sleep kept her under longer than it did Ethan or Gaston. She was barely a year dead. She needed her beauty sleep.

"All right. I've got this." She moved to the sofa and sat next to her charge. "Hi, Santa. Remember me? I saved your life last night."

"He needs to know the truth, dear Jane." Gaston steepled his fingers in the Magistrate's signature move, and Jane wondered if the old vampire gained strength with every new branch that was added to his family tree. If she wanted to use the family analogy, Gaston would be Santa's great-grandpa…but gross. Just imagining that made her shudder.

She thought back to how she felt when she woke up in Ethan's attic. Other than being disoriented and not remembering a damn thing at first, she'd felt like herself…just excruciatingly thirsty. So if Santa was nonstop laughing, this must have just been his jolly old self, right?

"Jane Devereaux." He patted his legs. "Why don't you sit on my lap and tell me what you want for Christmas?"

Her lip curled. "No thanks. I've seen what might pop up."

"You've seen…?" Ethan looked alarmed.

"Long story. Not what you think." She turned to Santa. "What's the last thing you remember?"

He stroked his beard, which was still stained red, and stared at the ceiling. The blood around his mouth and his biker clothes gave him a creepy horror-Christmas vibe, like he belonged in *The Gremlins*, not here. "I had some pralines, and then I went to Pat O'Brien's for a hurricane. They were playing my favorite song in the piano bar, so I had a few more before I left with Blitzen."

"Let me guess. Your favorite song is 'Santa Claus is Coming to Town'?" She snickered. Her first choice would have been "Rudolph the Red-Nosed Reindeer," but since he'd come to town on Blitzen, she didn't figure that was it.

"Ho, ho, *nope*. It's 'Grandma Got Run Over by a Reindeer.'"

"Oh, goat cheese." Jane guffawed. "That's your favorite song?"

Santa handed her a foil-wrapped cube. "It is."

"What's this?" She couldn't help the giggle rolling up from her throat. Santa-Fucking-Claus had just given her a present! How cool was that?

She peeled back the foil and found a white blob of something inside. Bringing the chunk to her nose, she took a whiff. "Is this goat cheese?"

Santa smiled proudly. "Exactly what you asked for."

She pursed her lips at the cheese.

"Not only is he a sugar fae," Gaston explained, "he's also a gifting fae. He and all the 'workshop elves' are."

"What are the air quotes for?" She set the gift on the coffee table.

"Workshop! Ho, ho, ho, there's no such place. We make all the gifts with magic. Ho, ho, ho. Ho, ho, ho." His ho's turned maniacal until he was cackling like a crazy man, and Jane made a *help me out here* face at Ethan.

Ethan lifted his shoulders. "You were out of sorts when you woke up, but you weren't insane."

Gaston let out an irritated grunt. "Vampires these days… You rely on your new-fangled technology—cellular phones and whatnot—when you should be using your instincts. Get your fledgling under control so we can take him to the Magistrate."

"What's his problem?" Jane sent her thoughts to Ethan's mind.

"I don't know, but I hope he pulls the candy cane out of his ass before your dad gets here."

"Ugh. Don't remind me about my dad. I can only handle one fiasco at a time."

"Touch him." Gaston shook his head like a disappointed father. "You and he share a connection. Physical contact will help him focus."

Jane started to put her hand on Santa's shoulder, but she hesitated. "Hold up a hot minute. When I was new—"

"You are still new, *ma chère*."

She rolled her eyes. "When I was new*er*, every time Ethan touched me, I wanted to rip his clothes off. That's not going to happen with Father Christmas, is it? Because I am not in the mood to fight off the sexual advances of a horny Santa."

"Ho, ho, ho. Ho, ho, ho." St. Nick continued his crazed laughter.

Gaston arched a brow. "He's a married man."

Jane matched his expression. "Your point?"

"I don't think you have to worry about that," Ethan said. "Not once in my entire undead existence have I felt the urge to see Gaston naked." He glanced at his sire. "No offense, man."

Gaston pressed a hand to his chest, feigning shock. "Not even once?"

"Sorry."

"Okay." Jane gripped Santa's shoulder. "Focus, Mr. Claus."

He snapped his head toward her, his eyes widening like he just remembered where he was.

"You got blitzed with Blitzen and left the bar. What happened next?"

"I needed to pee, so we stopped by a tree in the park. Then…" His lips pursed, drawing her attention to the bloodstains around his mouth. They'd have to clean him up before they took him to meet the Magistrate.

"I don't remember." He looked at her. "Do you have any soda? My throat feels like chestnuts roasting on an open fire."

"No, sorry." Jane cringed. She remembered the feeling, and there was only one thing that would tame the burn.

"Iced mocha? Sweet tea? Maple syrup?" His eyes grew wider and glassier with each question.

Jane glanced at Ethan before squaring her shoulders toward Santa. "You need blood."

"I'll settle for a glass of sugar water if that's all you've got."

"Santa…" She clutched his arm. "You're a vampire."

He blinked, tilting his head. "Don't be silly. *You're* a vampire. I'm king of the fae."

"You're both." She explained her little mishap behind the wheel. "If I hadn't turned you, you'd have died. So, now you're a hybrid—half-fae, half-vampire."

He stared straight ahead, stroking his blood-stained beard for what felt like forever but was probably only about thirty seconds. Then he looked at her and smiled. "I can live with that."

Ethan shifted in his seat. "Technically, you're not really living…"

"Too many details," she thought-spoke to her husband. Santa was cool with his predicament, so they needed to leave it alone.

Jane stood and tugged Santa to his feet. "Why don't you hop in the shower and give your beard a good scrub? You'll feel good as new, and I'll run your clothes through the wash before we meet the Magistrate."

"Can we stop for a milkshake on the way?" He followed her up the stairs to the bathroom.

"We'll see." Jane gestured to the shower. "Toss your clothes out after you undress, and I'll put them in the wash for you."

He shrugged out of his jacket, and she stepped down the hall to get a towel from the linen closet. When she returned, he'd already stripped down to his boxers, which matched his pin-up girl socks. *Not surprising.*

What Jane didn't expect was that all that bulk under his clothes was pure muscle. Seriously, the guy didn't seem to have an ounce of fat on his body. With his massive chest and abs she could do laundry on, he looked more like a polar bear shifter than a jolly old elf.

He caught her gawking and winked, but when he reached for the waistband of his undies, she shot into the hallway faster than a reindeer at feeding time—and those suckers were quick…she'd learned from experience!

"Ho, ho, here you go." He tossed his clothes into the hall and closed the bathroom door.

Jane gathered them up and threw them in the quick-wash cycle. As she closed the laundry room door, Santa's deep, melodious voice danced down the hall. Was he singing?

She tiptoed to the bathroom and pressed her ear against the door. Yep. He was singing.

> *Santa got run over by a vampire*
> *Peeing in the park on Christmas week.*
> *You may think there's no such thing as vampires,*
> *But as for me and Blitzen, we believe.*

Jane covered her mouth as she snorted. This guy was hilarious.

Half an hour later, his clothes were dry, and they were ready to go, but leaving blood on his snow-white beard all day had been a mistake. Even after his shower, he still had an orange stain around his mouth. There was nothing she could do about that now, though. They had an appointment with the Magistrate, and Jane needed to bring her A-game if she was going to get out of this alive…er… undead. Whatever.

CHAPTER FOUR

Ethan's knee bounced incessantly as they waited for the Magistrate to arrive. Jane rested her hand on his leg to still his fidgeting, but the other knee began bouncing instead. Santa sat in the leather chair on her opposite side, and Gaston stood in the corner, running his tongue over his fangs. They didn't have time to stop for breakfast on their way, not that they could have done much with Crazy Claus in tow.

A massive dark-wood desk sat in the center of the spacious office, and gothic renderings of famous and not-so-famous New Orleans landmarks decorated the space. Four metal filing cabinets occupied the far wall, and a foot-high stack of papers sat atop one of them, waiting for a new recruit to file them.

The Magistrate still liked his bookkeeping done old-school, but Jane was working on bringing the whole organization into the twenty-first century. If they'd ease up on their mandate that a vampire had to be dead for fifty years before they could run for a seat on the Council, she could get things done a lot faster, but that was a rule they wouldn't bend…not even for her.

Gaston had finagled a private appointment with the Magistrate, due to the elite status of the newest vampire in New Orleans, so they didn't have to appear before the entire Council…which was a very good thing. Jane may have had the Magistrate wrapped around her little finger, but the rest of the Volturi could suck it. Just forty-nine more years until she could infiltrate the patriarchy and really get shit done.

"Don't worry, babe. I've got this." She gave Ethan her most reassuring smile, even flashing a little fang because that always turned him on.

He took her hand, lacing his fingers through hers. His palm was colder than normal and a little clammy. "I know you do. That's not why I'm worried."

"What is it then?"

He fisted his free hand on his thigh and lowered his voice. "Your dad is coming the day after tomorrow."

She sighed. "Thanks for the reminder."

His nostrils flared as he blew out a breath, but seriously, it wasn't that big of a deal. Gaston was playing host since his house was bigger, so she and Ethan didn't have to do much to prepare. She'd made a shopping list for him, and they'd all agreed to no presents. They were good to go.

Santa took the stapler from the Magistrate's desk and squeezed it over and over, laughing as staples fell into his lap. "It's snowing!"

Jane snatched it away. "Don't touch anything." She turned to Ethan. *"The king of the fae is really not right in the head."*

"There does seem to be something off about him."

"That's an understatement."

"Ethan Devereaux's Christmas wish is the same as yours, Jane." Santa brushed the used staples onto the floor. "To be accepted by your father." He twisted in his seat to face them. "Are you sure I can't get you a pony?"

"Positive." She squeezed Ethan's hand. "Is that what you're worried about? That my dad won't accept you?"

"I did curse his only daughter to a life of darkness." His jaw worked as he ground his teeth, and Jane's heart melted. The smartest, most has-it-together vampire in all of New Orleans was scared to meet her father. How adorable.

"Aw. Don't you worry about Daddy. He's going to love you."

"How can you be so sure?"

"Because *I* love you. He'll see that. Maybe not right away, but he will." And she would keep telling herself that until she dropped the bomb on her poor old man. He would come around…eventually.

The Magistrate entered the office, and Jane and Ethan shot to their feet. She had to drag Santa up by the arm to get him to show their leader some respect. It seemed the king of the fae wasn't used to having superiors.

The Magistrate had piercing hazel eyes and long, dark hair woven into dreadlocks. Every time Jane looked at the man, he reminded her of Idris Elba, even now. He nodded, his lips curving into the tiniest of smiles as he caught Jane's gaze. *Oh, yeah. This will be easy.*

"Good evening, Magistrate," she said. "You're looking devilishly handsome, as always."

Ethan huffed, but he couldn't get mad at her. Flattery got you everything when it came to these ancient vampires.

"Good evening, dear Jane. Ethan, Gaston. I must get back to the Council meeting, so please, tell me about our newest recruit. Why does his registration require privacy?" His gaze locked on Santa, and recognition widened his eyes. "Is that…?"

"William Wonkers." Santa grinned. "Your Christmas wish is for the rest of the year to be as uneventful as possible so you can have a few days off to show Darius how much you appreciate him."

"And I can see that wish will not be coming true." He pursed his lips and glared at Jane.

She tried her best to keep a neutral expression. Honestly, she did, but she'd just found out the Magistrate…the supernatural leader of Louisiana…was named *William Wonkers*.

Her eyes watered as she held in her laughter. No wonder no one called him by his name. She expected him to be called something badass like Damon Steele or Kieran Sinclair or Constantine Augustus. Something fierce…

William Wonkers. She swallowed her snicker, wanting ever so badly to call him Willy Wonka, but she refrained. Her undead life was already on the line. Asking him about the Oompa Loompas would probably get her staked on the spot.

"So, I can explain all this, Your Honor. It was an honest mistake." Damn her lips for curving into a smile against her will.

The Magistrate glanced at the clock before sinking into his chair with a sigh. "Indeed you will, young Jane."

They all sat, and she told him about losing control of Genevieve, and how she turned Santa Claus into a vampire hybrid to save his life. "So, really, it's actually the same situation as when Ethan turned me, you see. I saved his life, so no harm was done."

The Magistrate did his signature finger steeple and cut his gaze between the four vampires. "And you were with her when this happened?" he asked Gaston, who straightened his spine.

"I was."

"As the senior vampire, I hold you partially responsible."

"I understand, sir." Gaston shot her the stink eye.

"And Ethan," the Magistrate continued, "as her sire, you are also responsible for her actions."

"Yes, sir. I shouldn't have left her unsupervised."

"Unsuper...?" Her mouth fell open, and she fought the urge to shoot to her feet. "They're not responsible for me in the slightest, Your Honor. I'm my own woman, and I take full blame for running over Santa."

"Santa got run over by vampire..." St. Nick sang.

"See?" She gestured to Santa. "Even he finds it amusing."

"My dear Jane." The Magistrate made a *tsk* sound as he shook his head. What was it with ancient vampires *tsking* at her lately? "There is nothing amusing about this situation, and you are overlooking one glaring difference between your situation and Ethan's when he turned you."

She remained silent, waiting for him to continue.

"Ethan didn't run you over. He truly did save your life. Santa's life wouldn't have needed saving if not for you; therefore, your actions were far from heroic. How will I explain his condition to the queen?"

Jane shrugged. "Aside from needing blood to survive, not much about him has changed. He already delivered presents during the night. He'll adjust."

Willy arched a brow. Hey, the Magistrate didn't have mind-reading abilities—that she knew of—so she could call him Willy in her head. "Not much has changed?" he asked. "Gaston, would you agree that not much has changed about Mr. Claus?"

Gaston shot Jane another look that sent chills down her spine. For the absolute first time in her undead life, she found the man intimidating. Scary, even. If Gaston the Drunk couldn't make light of the situation, maybe this was a whole lot worse than she imagined.

Santa sat beside her, gently rocking side-to-side while humming the tune to his favorite song. *Yep. A helluva lot worse.*

"It appears the transition from fae to hybrid has affected his brain. I've never seen him act quite so unhinged."

"I'd been drinking Pat O's hurricanes," Santa sang. "And I really had to pee. But I forgot I was in public. And so I drained my snake against a tree."

"Hell's bells," Ethan groaned. "Is he going to rewrite the entire song?"

"Merry Christmas!" Santa held an obsidian bell toward Ethan, darker than the darkest black she'd ever seen.

The Magistrate hissed. "Where did you get that?"

Jane suddenly felt entranced, and her hand reached toward the bell, almost of its own accord, but mostly because she wanted to ring that sucker more than she'd ever wanted to ring a bell in her entire life, including the little silver *ring bell for service* contraptions with the plunger you pressed to ding them. People got so annoyed when you rang those when they were already helping you.

Santa smiled proudly and shoved the bell toward Ethan again. "You're not on the naughty list. Take it."

Old Willy's eyes flashed red as he leaped over the desk and snatched the bell from Santa's hand. "Hell's bells will not ring in my coven." He stuffed a tissue inside the device to stop the chime from sounding.

Jane blinked, coming out of her trance. "That was an actual bell from literal hell? What would happen if it rang?"

"It would summon a demon," Willy said through clenched teeth as he glided around his desk.

"Psh." She waved off his reaction. "Demons aren't so bad." She'd been in a room full of them once. They'd tried to intimidate her, but she could've taken them all on, easy peasy.

Ethan squeezed her hand. "You've only met the recovering ones."

"True." And that succubus did seem fierce. She might have given Jane a run for her money.

The Magistrate opened a drawer, shoved the bell inside, and pulled out a sheet of paper. "Fill out his registration form. Get some blood in him, and we will hope to hell that solves the problem with his brain. I'd hate to see the fae queen's reaction if it doesn't."

Gaston visibly shuddered, and Ethan seemed to shrink inward. Jane didn't know much about the fae, but she had a feeling they weren't all fairy dust and lollipops based on her friends' reactions.

She scribbled Santa's information onto the form: First Name: Santa. Surname: Claus. Address? North Pole was good enough, right?

Willy…err…the Magistrate—she really needed to stop calling him that in her mind before she slipped and said it out loud—put his stamp of approval on the form and gave her a registration card for her charge.

He rose to his feet and moved so fluidly toward the door he seemed to float above the floor. "He will need to be licensed and sent back to the North Pole before Christmas Eve. Teach him quickly."

"Aye-aye, Captain. I mean, Your Honor." Jane saluted the Magistrate, and he paused in the doorway.

"And Jane, my dear. This really is your last strike. I appreciate everything you've done for the vampire community, but you've taken more than you've given. We've kept your undead condition a secret from the Texas Governor long enough. It's time to come clean, *and* take care of this problem…" He gestured to Santa, who still sat in his chair, swaying and humming. "Or there will be hell to pay."

A lump of hot coal lodged in her throat, foreshadowing how Christmas would go for her, perhaps? She nodded and swallowed it down as the Magistrate disappeared down the hall.

"Willy Wonka!" She slapped her hand over her mouth, trying her damnedest to hold in the fit of giggles threatening to escape. She could not break down in the coven house.

"Jane…" Ethan rubbed his temples.

"It must have taken incredible restraint for you to not say that in my presence," the Magistrate's voice drifted through her mind. *"I am confident you will clean up your mess before Christmas Eve. Do not let me down."*

She blew out a breath, her shoulders slumping in relief. "Good goat cheese pizza. That was a hoot, wasn't it?"

Santa held his hands palms up, and a ten-inch with ham appeared before her eyes.

"Thanks, buddy. Don't mind if I do." She picked up a

slice and took a bite. Human food had no nutritional value for the undead, but she'd be damned before she'd give up life's little pleasures. Especially if her undead days were numbered.

CHAPTER FIVE

Ethan shoved his hands in his pockets and walked a few paces behind Jane as they made their way into the French Quarter to look for Santa's first meal. His brow furrowed, and he looked every bit the brooding vampire he was when she first met him.

"What's wrong, babe?" She thought-spoke to avoid saying something that would trigger Santa to materialize a gift in front of the humans.

"Nothing," he grumbled. Yep, he was laying his Edward Cullen act on thick.

They crossed Bourbon Street, and, as expected, Gaston hung a left and disappeared into the crowd. That was fine. As long as Santa didn't faint at the sight of blood, teaching him to feed shouldn't be difficult. His throat had to be a desert full of cacti by now.

The scents of sage and incense filled the breeze as they passed Marie Laveau's House of Voodoo, and the symphony of music and laughter quieted as they drifted farther into the residential section of the Quarter.

Quaint Creole cottages painted in shades of blue and

yellow lined the street, their windows and porches adorned with tinsel and wreaths in December's signature colors. Santa smiled, revealing dimples and an impressive set of fangs. Good. He was thirsty.

"Santa got run over by a vampire…" he sang.

"Seriously, man. Can you come up with another song to sing?" she asked. "That one's getting old."

He rubbed his beard, looking thoughtful for a moment before he crooned, "On the first day of Christmas, a vampire ran over me, while I was peeing on a tree."

Jane lifted her hands in the air and dropped them at her sides. "I give up."

Ethan looked so tense, you could have cracked a chestnut between his butt cheeks and roasted it in his glowering gaze.

She'd sensed he was stressed ever since they decided to invite her dad over for Christmas, and she understood now why he was nervous, but damn. It really wasn't *that* big of a deal. There had to be something else bothering him.

She stepped between two houses, disappearing into the shadows and tugging Santa back with her. "Focus on being invisible. That's the first lesson in vampire glamour. Blend in, so the humans don't suspect they're about to become a meal."

Santa winked and disappeared.

"Wow. You're a fast learner. Even I can't see through your glamour." She touched his arm, and the magical veil dissolved from her view.

"He's using fae glamour," Ethan said. "The only thing you'll need to teach him is how to bite without hurting and how to seal the wounds."

"That makes my job a whole helluva lot easier. Now,

we just wait for someone to walk by." She reached for Ethan's hand, but he kept it shoved in his pocket.

She sighed. *"Really, Ethan. Tell me what's on your mind. Maybe I can help?"*

He locked his brooding gaze with hers, and his jaw clenched. *"I'm nervous about meeting your dad."*

"I know, but it seems like there's something more."

He ground his teeth, hesitating to go on, so she batted her lashes, imploring him with her gaze.

"I haven't had a happy Christmas in twenty-five years, and I was looking forward to spending this one with you and our friends. Now, we're coming clean to your dad and dealing with this." He waved a hand at Santa, who waved back. *"It's not the Christmas I was hoping for."*

Well, damn. She'd forgotten how miserable Ethan had been before they met. Her bright idea to have her dad over had made him anxious enough, and now they had Sanity-Impaired Santa to deal with on top of it all.

Jane hadn't saved Christmas. She'd ruined it for the one person who meant the most.

"I'll call him and cancel. I can say I've come down with the flu." She linked her arm around his. *"He thinks I'm human, so he'll believe it."*

"No. We need to tell him. We should have told him when we were in Texas last month."

The boys had driven her to see the High Priestess of the Texas coven of witches to acquire a potion her best friend Sophie had needed. Jane briefly saw her father then, but she'd left Ethan and Gaston behind, not ready to deal with the fallout of telling him that not only was she a vampire, but she'd gotten married without his blessing.

Yeah, yeah. She was a strong, independent woman and

didn't need her dad's permission to get married, but still…
"I'll make it up to you. I promise."

"Just get Santa licensed and out of the house before your dad arrives. That's all I want."

"Right." She could do that. But she *would* make it up to Ethan one way or another.

"Dinner approaching. Three o'clock." He nodded toward a couple heading their way.

"Okay, Santa. We're going to hypnotize them. Use your glamour to sorta blank her mind, and then pull her into the shadows. I'll get the man."

Santa used glamour like a pro, thanks to the fact he already had these powers before he was turned. With the couple successfully zombified, Jane demonstrated proper biting technique and showed him how to seal the wounds with magical vampire saliva. Then, she showed him how to place a meal mark on the target, which was the only new bit of glamour he had to learn.

"Now it's your turn." She passed the man to Ethan, who kept him from wandering off before she could remove the trance.

Santa looked at the woman's neck and leaned down, pressing his nose to her skin. His lip curled in disgust as he pulled back and shoved her away. "She smells like copper and salt."

"That's what blood smells like," Jane said. "Just take a sip and try it."

"I want a milkshake." He stamped his foot like a spoiled child.

"Oh, for fuck's sake." She threw her arms in the air. "You're a vampire now. You need blood to survive."

"A milkshake or an iced peppermint mocha." He crossed his arms like a stubborn snowman.

Ethan suppressed a chuckle behind her, and she spun around to face him. "What's so funny, mister?"

He laughed. "Karma's a bitch, isn't it?"

She parked her hands on her hips. "I had a psychological condition that made it impossible for me to feed. He's just being a big baby."

"Well…no sense wasting a decent meal." Ethan stepped toward the woman and sank his fangs into her neck. When he was done, they lifted the trance and sent the couple on their way.

"We've got to get some blood in him." He shoved his hands back into his pockets and paced down the sidewalk. Jane jogged to catch up, but Santa just strolled along, admiring the holiday decorations.

"Do you have any ideas? You managed to get me drinking blood, even if it wasn't from the vein at first."

He shook his head. "That was all Sophie. She knew you better than me. She knew what it would take to get you to drink." He stopped walking and glanced back at Santa. "We may need to call Mrs. Claus now."

Jane gawked. "Mrs. Claus, as in the fae queen? The one whose mere mention made a three-hundred-year-old vampire shake in his boots? I saw the way y'all reacted when the Magistrate talked about her. Uh-uh. No way. We're not calling her until he's licensed and ready to go."

"Christmas Eve is three days away."

"Then we'd better hurry. Come on, I have an idea." She led them down a side street back toward the commercial end of the French Quarter. By the time they reached their destination, Santa was stumbling like a tourist on his first trip to Bourbon Street, though he hadn't had a drop of alcohol since he woke up dead.

Jane supported his weight on one side, while Ethan

propped up the other, and they practically had to *Weekend at Bernie's* him down the alley between the ice cream parlor and the praline shop.

"I wasn't this bad off my first night, was I?" She unwrapped Santa's arm from around her shoulders and leaned him against the wall.

"He's deteriorating much more quickly than you did." Ethan held him upright by the bicep. "Exponentially faster, and a milkshake isn't going to do him a lick of good."

She hovered near the front of the alley, waiting for someone to step outside the shop. "We're not getting him a milkshake...just the blood of someone on a sugar high."

"That's a good idea," Ethan said. "His sugar fae side is probably starving too."

"Exactly." Jane locked her gaze on two petite women exiting the ice cream shop. They'd just shared a massive banana split and washed it down with sodas. *Perfect.*

She turned on her glamour full blast and lured them into the alley. They only needed one, but it was easier to put them both in a trance than to have one run off screaming about the monsters in the shadows.

"All right, Kris Kringle, this one should smell a lot better." She positioned the brunette in front of Santa, angling her head so he could easily reach her neck.

"Jingle bells, werewolves smell, a vampire ran me down," he sang to the tune of "Jingle Bells."

"That's seriously getting old." And Jane was starting to understand why Ethan was such a Grumpy McGrumpy Pants when he was teaching her the ways of the vampire. Being responsible for another person's livelihood was hard work and no fun...which was exactly why she'd never wanted to have children. She didn't have a motherly bone in her body.

"Here's the vein. Pierce and suck. Then lick the wounds," she said.

Santa pressed his nose to the woman's neck and inhaled deeply. Jane held her breath, crossing her fingers and her toes, praying to every god, spirit, and sprite in existence that the man would drink. They didn't have time for him to pull a Jane Anderson and refuse for weeks.

"Do you mind?" Ethan's fangs were fully extended as he watched the other woman, who leaned her back against the wall and stared blankly ahead.

"Go ahead, babe." Devil knew he deserved a midnight snack more than she did.

Santa glanced at Ethan as he fed from the woman, and old St. Nick's vampire instinct finally took control. His pupils constricted, and he peeled back his lips to reveal fully-formed, frighteningly long fangs. It was a good thing he didn't visit human children anymore. Vampire Santa would surely give them nightmares.

He pierced the vein like a pro, groaning as he fed. When he pulled back, he looked even drunker than before, but that was normal. It would take a second or two for the blood to revive him.

She taught him how to seal the wounds, and then they practiced the glamour tactics for making sure his meals never remembered the service they performed before sending the women on their way.

"Feeling better?" she asked.

"Like the star on top of a Christmas tree."

"Okay…" Was that a good thing? She wasn't sure. His eyes seemed more coherent, so she'd call it a win.

"I spoke with someone at the coven house," Ethan said

as he stuffed his phone into his pocket. "If we get there fast, they can squeeze him in for a licensing appointment."

"Perfect. Then we'll call Mrs. Claus, explain that everything is okay, and she can come get him tomorrow night...with plenty of time to get ready for Christmas Eve." See, she knew it would all work out.

And it did...at first.

Santa passed his licensing exam easy peasy, and for the first half of the walk back to their house in Marigny he seemed like his jolly old self.

Then he started humming Christmas tunes. No big deal, right? He was Santa Claus. If Jane had albums full of songs written about her, she'd probably walk around humming them too.

But then his walking turned to stumbling; the humming led to singing, and... "Santa got run over by a vampire."

Jane groaned. "Not again."

Santa stopped walking and swayed, his eyes rolling backward as his words slurred.

"Just a few more blocks, big guy." Ethan supported his weight on one side; Jane took the other, and they carried him. Again.

"His body processed the blood way too fast. His fae side must be messing with his vampire." Ethan unlocked the front door, and they settled Santa on the dark blue couch.

Jane stood in front of the oak entertainment center and looked at the deteriorating vamp/fae, tapping a finger to her lips. "Can you run to the corner store and buy a bag of sugar? I think a miracle cure is in order."

While Ethan ran out to the store, she microwaved a bottle of blood and poured it into a mug. When he returned, she mixed in as much sugar as she could get to dissolve in the thick liquid and then offered the mug to Santa.

He tilted his head. "Hot cocoa?"

"Even better. It's called a miracle cure. You'll be feeling like your old self in no time." *I hope.*

Ethan took a bag of carrots from the fridge. "Gaston brought Blitzen over here. I'm going out to check on him."

"Don't be long. Morning's coming." She smiled at her husband, but he just nodded and headed for the back door. His lips didn't even twitch.

Cheese and crackers. She had *a lot* of making up to do.

Santa chugged the blood, staining his mustache yet again. She should have given him a straw. After having him wash his face and take off his boots, she got him tucked into bed in the guest room. The death sleep pulled him under the moment his head hit the pillow, and Jane let out a sigh of relief. At least she'd get half an hour alone with her husband before the sleep pulled her under too.

She walked out to the backyard and found Ethan there, stroking Blitzen's nose and whispering something to the reindeer. If she focused, her vampire super hearing would have allowed her to make sense of what he said, but at this point…she didn't want to know.

"Hey, you." She rested a hand on his shoulder and kissed his cheek.

"He's magnificent, isn't he?" Ethan didn't look at her. Instead, he pressed his forehead to the deer's, right below the antlers.

"He certainly is." She tried to ignore the sting of rejection poking her in the chest.

"And you got to ride him. Lucky." He chuckled.

"When I was kid, every time I'd go to the mall to sit on fake Santa's lap, when he asked what I wanted for Christmas, I always said I wanted to ride a reindeer."

"Why don't you take him for a quick spin around the block?"

Ethan shook his head. "The sun will be up soon. I'd rather not risk becoming barbeque." Always the cautious one, her husband.

"Santa's probably having visions of sugarplums by now. Want to see how many white Christmases we can get in before I get sucked under?"

He pursed his lips as he finally looked into her eyes. Cupping her cheek in his hand, he leaned in and kissed her forehead. "Not tonight, princess. I'm tired."

Ouch.

CHAPTER SIX

"What, exactly, did you say to her when you called?" Willy the Magistrate sat in a dark blue recliner, looking regal in his black robes with his dreadlocks pulled back into a band at the nape of his neck.

There was no such thing as a vampire king, even though the head of the Supernatural World Order did call himself the Emperor. Vamps ran themselves with elected officials, and each territory, AKA "dominion"—because didn't that sound so much more menacing?—had a Magistrate who reported directly to the Emperor.

Lucky for Jane, this Magistrate not only liked her but also liked to take care of his people and his dominion without the SWO's interference. He could have reported her mishap with Santa straight to the top. Instead, he was about to meet with the fae queen to help Jane explain why her sugary-sweet husband would fry in the sunlight for the rest of his undead existence.

She slipped her hand into Ethan's for support, expecting his words of encouragement to dance through her mind. He held her hand, but he didn't thought-speak —or regular-speak—a single syllable.

Fantastic. Thanks to her shenanigans, her husband was mad at her, the Magistrate was mad at her, and now the queen of the fae was about to be royally pissed.

At least Gaston had stayed home to get his house ready for their guests, so she didn't have to deal with getting the stink eye from him.

She cleared her throat. "I told her that her husband was here and that he was safe, but she needed to meet with our Magistrate before we could send him home."

"And what was her response?" He steepled his fingers.

"She growled. At least…it sounded like a growl, and then she said she'd be here in two shakes of a reindeer's tail."

Santa sang to the tune of "Jingle Bells" yet again, "Magistrate, my wife is late, a vampire ran me down."

"Satan's balls, man." Jane raked her fingers through her hair. "Would you stop with the Christmas song parodies?"

Santa laughed. "Satan's balls? I've never had that request before, but I'll see what I can do. I've heard he has quite a collection."

"No!" all three of them shouted in unison.

Hell's bells. The last thing they needed was for the lord of the underworld to show up demanding they return his testicles.

"Devil's nuts roasting on an open fire…" he sang. "Jack Frost sucking on your—"

"Here, Santa." Jane shoved a mug in his face. "Have another cup of sugar blood before your wife gets here."

"It's rather unnerving." The Magistrate leaned forward, studying Santa as he gulped down the blood. "I've seen a few vampire-fae hybrids, but they were all completely sane."

"Have you ever turned a fae, sir?" Ethan asked. "Is there something Jane needs to do differently?"

"Oh, sure. Blame it on me." She narrowed her eyes.

"You are the reason he's in this condition."

She huffed and crossed her arms. *"Why do you always have to be right?"*

"It's disrespectful to use telepathy in the presence of your superiors." The Magistrate cut his gaze between them, scolding them with his eyes, and they both hung their heads.

"Sorry," Jane muttered.

"I have never turned a fae, and I'm afraid no one in the vicinity has either. The fae keep to themselves, staying away from cities and other supes. Hybrids are rare, but I've never heard of the transformation affecting anyone's brain like this."

"Great." Jane clutched her hands in her lap. "So we're turning over a crazy man to the queen of the fae."

The Magistrate shuddered, and Ethan straightened his spine, tensing.

"Damn. She must be one helluva ball-buster to get you guys so worked up. Mrs. Claus isn't going to turn us into snowmen and plow us into the ground, is she?"

Ethan shook his head. "I've never met the woman, but I've heard stories."

"Like?" she asked.

"She can be rather…outspoken." The Magistrate rubbed his chin with his thumb and forefinger. "She's not unlike someone else I know."

Ethan arched a brow at Willy, and they had their own thought-speak conversation, leaving Jane out. She started to protest, but honestly, she didn't need to know what they were saying. Obviously that *outspoken* someone else was her.

A knock sounded on the door, and Ethan and the Magistrate shot to their feet, while Santa played with his empty mug, pretending to drink from it before turning it over and over in his hands, only to fake drink again.

Jane slowly rose and strode toward the door. "Why don't you let me talk to her first? I'll break the news and then bring her inside to see the damage."

Willy stiffened. "She's the queen. She needs to be met with respect worthy of her rank, or she will make our lives an undead hell."

Jane rested a hand on her hip. "She's a woman who needs to be met with respect period. I've got this."

"I believe we should trust her, Your Honor." Ethan nodded at Jane. *"You've never let me down before."*

"Damn straight." Her husband might have been pissed at her for taking the happy out of his holidays, but at least he still believed in her. She kissed his cheek and gripped the doorknob, waiting for the Magistrate's permission. Hey, she'd pissed the man off enough. She knew when to stop pushing her luck.

"Very well, but if the discussion gets heated, you will let us know so we can assist."

"Got it." *Like you won't be listening with your ears to the door anyway.* She turned around before they could see her eyeroll and bit her tongue to keep from insisting she wouldn't need their *assistance.* Truth be told, she might.

Opening the door a crack, she slipped through and closed it behind her, bracing herself as she faced the woman who struck fear into the hearts of men.

Mrs. Claus wore a tight, red corset with white fur trim

across the top, red leggings, and tall, black boots with three-inch heels. Long, white hair cascaded around her shoulders, and a poinsettia was pinned above her left ear.

Yep, she was the pin-up girl on Santa's socks. *I wonder if Ethan would wear socks with pictures of a scantily-clad me...?* She shook her head. *Focus on the Claus, girlie.*

The woman didn't look a day over thirty, and she was plump in all the right places. Why Jane was expecting a squat, little old lady, she wasn't sure. Aside from the beard, Santa looked nothing like his pop culture renderings, so why should Mrs. Claus? She stood about five-foot-nine and had the graceful elegance of a ballerina, with a resting bitch face that could freeze hell with a pointed look. Hopefully the queen of the fae wouldn't be a royal pain in the ass.

"Hello, Queen Claus." She curtsied because what else were you supposed to do in front of a monarch? Kiss her feet? Tap dance to "Winter Wonderland"? Jane had never met royalty in her life—supe or human. She should have asked the Magistrate for a crash course in fae etiquette.

Mrs. Claus's bitch face melted away, her brows pinching as worry tightened her lavender eyes. "Where is he? I need to see him. Is he...okay?" She tapped her temple.

Wait a minute... Was she implying he wasn't "okay" before Jane ran him over? *Well, I'll be a snowman's uncle.* That would explain why he'd decided to stop for a pee against a tree in the first place. No one in his right mind— vamp, fae, or otherwise—would whip out his Yule log in City Park.

"He's inside, Your Majesty, and I'll take you to see him. But there's something you need to know before we go in."

"Is he still singing and randomly materializing gifts related to everything you say?"

Jane couldn't stop the relieved giggle from escaping her lips. She wasn't responsible for Santa's broken brain! Halleluiah! "Yes, yes, he is."

"But he's alive." She threw her arms around Jane and gave her the biggest bear hug she'd ever received. Not surprisingly, she smelled of peppermint and marzipan… like Christmas. "Thank you for keeping him safe."

Jane patted her back. "He's safe, but the alive part is debatable."

Mrs. Claus pulled back, her brow furrowing. "What do you mean?"

"Funny story…" Jane forced a laugh. Was this the part where the queen unleashed her fae magic, choking her to death with fairy dust and a candy cane through the heart? Time to find out…

"Santa got hit by a car. He was caroling on death's door, so I kinda sorta might have turned him into a vampire to save him." She cringed, steeling herself for the fury.

Mrs. Claus blinked rapidly, her expression incredulous. "My husband is…a vampire?"

"He's a hybrid. He still has all his fae powers. Really, the only difference now is that he needs to drink blood, and he can't go out in the sunlight."

Her red lips parted as she shook her head. "My husband is a vampire."

"I'm really sorry. I didn't mean to run him over. I lost control of the car, and he was standing so close to the road… But he's okay! He's up and about and feeding like a pro. The tinsel doesn't go all the way to the top of his tree, but it sounds like he was already a few berries short of a complete wreath before it happened."

"You're the one who ran him over?" Her expression turned unreadable. It wasn't a bitch face or an angry face, but it wasn't an *everything is going to be okay* face either.

Jane was beginning to understand why the guys were shaking in their boots. Was she mad? Was she sad? Was she hungry? It was impossible to tell. "I am, and I am so, so sorry." She readied her thought-speak to call for help.

Mrs. Claus inhaled deeply, stepping back and leaning against the porch railing. One corner of her mouth twitched, and her eyes softened. "You know the fae are immortal, right?"

Jane opened her mouth, but she hesitated to speak. It sounded like a trick question...or maybe it was rhetorical. When she didn't respond, the queen arched a brow, expecting an answer.

"I thought y'all were, but I could sense Santa's life slipping away." Why did she feel like she was pleading for her own life? "My friend Gaston felt it too, and he's ancient, so he knows what's what. I wouldn't have done it if I'd thought he would recover."

She was silent for a moment, her gaze fixed on something in the distance over Jane's shoulder, but Jane didn't dare turn around to see what it was. "There are few things that can kill a fae. Iron, of course, is a weakness for all of us, but for the sugar fae, the most dangerous substance is sucralose."

Jane tilted her head. "The artificial sweetener? Isn't it made from sugar?"

"It is, but the chlorination process contaminates the molecules, turning it poisonous to the fae who rely on sugar to fuel their bodies."

"Wow. And I thought aspartame was bad for you." She stepped toward Mrs. Claus and leaned her hip against the railing. Being so familiar around royalty might not have been the best idea, but Jane refused to cower in fear. "Are you saying you think Santa was poisoned, and that's why he was dying?"

Mrs. Claus pursed her lips and gazed upward as if she were holding back tears. "I *know* he was poisoned, and, yes, that's why he was dying." She swallowed hard and looked Jane in the eyes. "Your accident happened at just the right time. Sucralose has no effect on vampires, so by turning my husband into a hybrid, you saved his life. Thank you, Jane."

Her breath of relief came out in a whoosh. *Thank goat cheese!* "I'm glad I could help." She sent her thoughts to both Ethan and the Magistrate. *"You hear that, boys? I really did save Santa's life."*

"Indeed, you did, dear Jane," Willy said. *"Perhaps I should speak with her now."*

"Give me a minute. We're bonding." She turned to the queen. "If you don't mind my asking, what happened to him?"

"A coup. Barnaby, once our most trusted head elf, decided he'd had enough of our holiday cheer. He's been slowly poisoning my husband, replacing the sugar in his cocoa with sucralose a little at a time so he didn't notice."

Jane gaped. "Wow."

She blew out a disgusted breath. "Tell me about it. He thought with Santa out of the way, he could marry me and become king of the fae. I'm sure I'd have been next on his hit list after he claimed the title."

Who knew life at the North Pole would be like living in a soap opera? "That rat bastard."

"By the time we figured out what was happening and who the culprit was, Santa's mind had deteriorated. Then he went missing. He left his phone and Blitzen's tracking halter at home, so he could have been anywhere in the world."

A sad smile curved the queen's lips. "I should have known he'd come here. He's always had a soft spot for your pralines."

Jane nodded. Relieved didn't even begin to describe how she felt. "So, we're cool then? You're not mad that I turned your husband into a vampire?"

"Are you kidding? Ever since that *Interview with a Vampire* movie, I've had a secret fantasy about them."

She laughed. "Really?"

"When your sole purpose is to spread love and joy, a taste of forbidden darkness can be tempting. If his mind comes back, you'll have made my wildest dreams come true."

Hot damn! Who was the spreader of Christmas cheer now? "Are you ready to come inside and see him?"

She nodded. "I am, but I do have one question before we go in."

"Shoot."

She pressed her lips together, glancing at the door before focusing on Jane. "I assume your Magistrate is inside. Why did he send you out to speak with me first?"

"He didn't. This was my idea."

"Why?"

Jane shrugged. "All the guys are afraid of you, but I had a feeling you were just misunderstood."

She pushed from the railing, shifting her weight to one foot and resting her hand on her hip. "When a man is outspoken and stands up for himself, he's called a good leader, an alpha. When a woman acts the same way, she's labeled a bitch."

"You're a threat to the patriarchy." Jane laughed. No wonder the entire Vampire Council was scared of the woman. It was the same reason none of them—except for ole Willy himself—liked Jane.

"Precisely."

"You and me both, Mrs. Claus. Only forty-nine more years until I can run for a seat on the Council."

"You'll have the backing of the fae when you do. And please…call me Cindy."

"Hell yeah!" Jane held up her hand for a high-five—which probably wasn't the smartest thing to do to a queen—but Cindy didn't leave her hanging. She slapped her palm, and a puff of iridescent powder sparkled around their hands before drifting to the ground like snow. No, not snow…fairy dust. *So cool!*

"Do you need to park your rein…deer…?" Jane looked into the driveway, expecting to find another deer disguised as a Harley, but nothing was there.

"I don't need the deer to travel. I can fly." Right before her eyes, Cindy unfurled a pair of glistening white wings covered in shimmering snowflakes. They sparkled in the porch light, and as she flapped them, the scents of peppermint and marzipan encircled Jane, reminding her of Christmases with her mom long ago.

"Wow." What more could she say? The woman was magnificent. "Um…come on in." Jane opened the door and led Cindy inside.

Santa sat on the couch with his back to the entrance, so he didn't see his wife when she walked in. Cindy paused and tucked her wings away, sadness tightening her eyes as he mumbled incoherently to the tune of "Santa Claus is Coming to Town."

She looked at the Magistrate. "I assume, with your enhanced hearing, you heard our conversation, and there is no need to rehash the details?"

"You are correct, madam, and may I say what a pleasure it is to see you again." He bowed formally, and Jane held back a laugh. The supernatural leader of Louisiana was afraid of a Christmas fairy. What a hoot!

"This is my husband, Ethan." She slipped her hand into his as he nodded a hello.

"You've landed yourself a keeper, young man," Cindy said. "Treat her right."

"Yes, ma'am. I will."

"Fair warning." Jane touched Cindy's arm as she started toward Santa. "He's got a bit of a blood mustache since we were feeding him from a mug."

She nodded and strode around the sofa to face her husband. He looked at her, but not a trace of recognition sparked in his eyes as he launched into his dreaded "Santa Got Run Over by a Vampire" routine.

Jane stood between Ethan and Willy, holding her breath and hoping against hope that seeing his soulmate would jog Santa's memory and derail his crazy train.

"Santa?" Cindy sank onto the couch next to him and rested her hand on his knee. "Sugar plum, are you ready to come home for Christmas?"

"I'll be dead for Christmas…" he sang.

Ethan put his free hand on Jane's arm, and she let out a breath, glancing at their entwined fingers. She'd been squeezing his hand so tight, her knuckles had turned white —which said a lot when a pale-as-a-snowman's-ass vampire turned even paler. *C'mon, Kris Kringle. You've got to bring joy to the world soon.*

"Santa, baby. It's Cindy. Look at me." She cupped his cheek in her hand, turning his face toward her.

He tilted his head, and for a hot minute, Jane thought he recognized his wife. But when he inhaled, his lips parting as his fangs elongated, it was clear he recognized food, and not the woman he loved.

"Cindy." He brushed her hair behind her shoulder, exposing her neck, and leaned toward her.

Jane's weight shifted to her toes as if she planned to stop him, but he was a vampire for goat cheese's sake. The man had to eat.

It was a good thing she didn't stop him, because as he sank his fangs into his wife's neck, she let out an erotic moan to rival the most seasoned porn star. She clutched his shoulders, closing her eyes and smiling like she enjoyed being Santa's snack. Had he even glamoured her? It didn't seem like it.

Jane straightened her spine, smiling proudly as Santa licked the wounds, sealing them and erasing any trace of a puncture. She felt a little like a mom who'd just watched her firstborn graduate from high school.

Santa pulled back, and the cray-cray look his eyes had held since she met him dissolved. His pupils constricted to a normal size, and his smile looked like the jolly mall Santa you took your picture with, not the creepy guy ringing the bell outside Walmart.

"Cindy, my gumdrop." He tucked her hair behind her ear. "Christmas would have been blue without you."

Taking her face in his hands, he kissed her. Hard. They made out on the couch for an awkwardly long time until

Jane finally cleared her throat, drawing Cindy's attention. "Is he okay now?"

She smiled, and an honest-to-goat-cheese twinkle formed in her eye. "He's perfect."

"You are one steaming-hot mug of wassail, my peppermint." Santa stood, pulling Cindy to her feet and wrapping his arms around her, planting another ginormous kiss on her lips.

Jane cocked her head, chewing her bottom lip. That was it? The king of the fae just needed to see his wife, and he was saved by true love's kiss? Nah. The thought was romantic, but that couldn't possibly be what happened.

"Oh…" Jane bumped the heel of her hand to her forehead. "We were giving him the wrong kind of blood."

"Of course." Ethan shook his head. "We used to be human, so we need human blood to survive. Santa used to be fae."

"So he needs fae blood, duh."

Ethan let out a dry laugh. "I can't believe we didn't figure that out."

Willy arched a brow. "Nor can I."

Whoops. Oh, well. Santa now had his own personal— and judging by the way her fingers dug into his butt cheeks as they made out—more-than-willing food supply.

"Mmm, Cindy." Santa clutched her leg, lifting it over his hip and grabbing her by the ass. She jumped and cinched her legs around his waist before he pressed her against the wall and groped her.

"Oh my." Jane shielded her eyes for a moment, but then she peeked through her fingers as Cindy's corset hit the floor. *Holy crap.* Mr. and Mrs. Claus were getting it on in her living room. "Umm… Maybe we should step outside?"

His pants hit his ankles, and Jane made a beeline for the door. *Santa Claus is Coming to Town* just took on a whole new meaning. "Beans and rice! I guess royalty can screw anywhere they want?"

"His reaction is quite normal for a fledgling vampire." The Magistrate walked down the front steps onto the sidewalk.

Jane stopped on the porch, but when the moaning inside intensified, she and Ethan joined him for a short walk down the street. "I don't remember being that horny when I was turned," she said.

Ethan chuckled. "You said every time I touched you that you wanted to rip my clothes off."

"Oh, yeah." She grinned. "I still feel that way."

"Imagine if we had already been in love when I turned you."

"I'd have devoured you." She licked her lips. "You wouldn't have been able to walk when I got through with you."

"Jane, dear," Willy said. "I apologize for scolding you about using telepathy in front of me. Some things should not be said aloud."

"Sorry about that, Will…err…Your Honor."

They took a lap around the block to give the Clauses some privacy, and when they returned, Santa stepped onto the porch. Cindy followed, adjusting her boobs in her corset and grinning like…well, like a woman who'd just had the best lay of her life.

"Feeling better, Santa?" Jane walked up the steps and leaned against the railing.

"Ho, ho, ho. I'm a new man, thanks to you." He tugged Cindy to his side. "And you won't believe how happy my wife is with my new vampire prowess, right, cherry pie?"

Cindy flashed Jane a knowing smile. "I'm sure she's well aware."

"William." Santa shook the Magistrate's hand. "I am beyond impressed with your subjects. In my moment of insanity, I couldn't have been in better hands. You have an ally in the fae for life."

Willy bowed. "Thank you, sir. They are both assets to our organization."

Assets, huh? Jane would have to remind the Magistrate he said that the next time he threatened to have her staked, which, knowing her, would be next week.

"Are you sure I can't bring you a pony?" Santa winked at Jane, and she shook her head. "I believe your friend Gaston will find his Christmas wish has come true, then."

"Let me guess…Genevieve?"

"She's as good as new."

"Jane." Cindy linked arms with her and led her down the steps to the sidewalk as Santa went around back to get his reindeer. "If you ever need anything, please don't hesitate to ask. Anything at all."

She glanced at Ethan standing on the porch with the Magistrate. "There is one thing you could do for me." She waited until the fae glamour made Blitzen sound like a revving engine before whispering her request to Cindy.

Mrs. Claus's lavender eyes glinted as she smiled. "That can be arranged."

"Awesome."

"Thank you again for everything." Cindy waved goodbye and climbed onto the back of Blitzen. Then, Santa and Mrs. Claus rode off into the distance.

Jane couldn't fight her grin as she pranced up the porch steps. "I told you it would all work out."

Ethan's smile wasn't very convincing. The tension in his shoulders had eased a bit, but her father's visit loomed right around the corner. They weren't out of the haunted woods yet.

"Tomorrow will be just as easy." She hoped. Truth be told, she wasn't sure how her dad would react to the bomb they were about to drop on him, and even she was getting nervous the closer they got to impact.

"I hope you're right."

She kissed his cheek. "I have an idea. Let's go inside, and I'll help you relieve some of that stress. We've got a few hours before sunrise. Wanna see how many snowballs I can make Vlad throw?"

The Magistrate cleared his throat. "That would be another example of an appropriate use of telepathy."

"Sorry."

Willy clasped his hands behind his back. "I'm afraid you'll need to come to the coven house with me. We have paperwork to fill out."

Jane scoffed. "Paperwork? Seriously?"

"You turned the king of the fae into a vampire. We'll need a written account of every detail for the record books."

"Can't I email it to you in a few days?" A romp in the sheets with her man sounded way more fun than paperwork. Hell, having her fangs pulled would have been more fun.

"Come on." Ethan took her hand and tugged her toward the sidewalk. "We can have a snowball fight another time… If your father doesn't stake me at first sight."

CHAPTER SEVEN

E than sat in the driver's seat of his Ford Taurus, but he didn't start the ignition. Jane watched him from the corner of her eye as he gripped the steering wheel, the tendons in his neck so taut, they might snap at any second. Forget about cracking a chestnut between his butt cheeks. Right now, he could probably make a diamond.

"Are you ready to go?" She cupped the back of his neck, attempting to rub the tension from his muscles, but he was as tight as a reindeer's ass in a snowstorm.

"Yeah." He pressed the start button and reached for the gear shifter.

"Hold on." Jane put her hand on top of his, not allowing him to shift the car into drive.

"Your father is waiting for us," he said through clenched teeth.

"Okay, this has gone on long enough." She crossed her arms over her chest. "I get that you're nervous about meeting him, but there is something else going on with you. Please, for the love of goat cheese, tell me what's wrong."

His jaw worked like he was grinding his teeth, and he cut his gaze toward her before staring out the windshield. "It's nothing."

"It's obviously something. You weren't even strung this tight when we were both facing the stake at the hands of that twit constable back in March. Mr. Broody McBroody Pants needs to take a hike and let my caring, sensitive husband have a conversation with the woman who loves him more than anything in the world."

He swallowed hard, his posture deflating as he turned toward her. His mouth opened and closed like he was trying to find the words, and his nostrils flared as he blew out a breath. "I've never gone with a woman to meet her parents before."

She started to laugh but thought better of it. Surely there was more to it. There had to be. And anyway... "You were engaged. You never met Vanessa's parents?"

He squared his gaze on her. "They lived in Connecticut. The first time I met them was when they came to New Orleans to take her body home."

"Oh, I see." Why the hell didn't he tell her this before? She'd have tried a little harder to ease his fears if she'd known what a big deal this was to him. Now she felt like a big ole bitch for not taking his anxiety seriously.

"Their daughter was dead, and they blamed me," he said. "You are undead, and your father will blame me too. Forgive me if that's a genre of music I'm not ready to face again."

"He won't blame you." She gave his shoulder a squeeze. "I wouldn't even be here if it weren't for you."

"You wouldn't have wandered down that side street and gotten run over if you hadn't sensed me watching you."

She took his hand, lacing her fingers through his. "And if I wasn't the hottest piece of eye candy to ever grace New Orleans with her presence, you wouldn't have been watching me."

He chuckled.

"What happened, happened," she said. "Whether it was fate, an accident, or just my lucky day, it doesn't matter. I'm happy, and I love you. He'll see that, and he'll love you too."

"And if he doesn't?"

She lifted one shoulder in a dismissive shrug. "We've avoided seeing him for ten months now. We can go another ten if he wants to throw a fit."

Ethan's eyes tightened, so Jane stroked his cheek with the back of her hand.

"He won't throw a fit. Not a big one, anyway. Just let me do the talking, and we'll ease him into it. At least he already knows vampires are real, so we can skip the trying to convince him stage." While supes kept their existence a secret from most humans, those high up in government—like her dad—knew about them. How he *felt* about them, she had no clue.

One corner of Ethan's mouth tugged up into an almost-smile. "Okay, princess. Let's do this."

They drove down Decatur Street through the French Quarter, past the Central Business District, and into the Garden District. Twinkling lights and holiday décor accented the windows and eaves of the businesses and homes, and people milled about in the evening moonlight, heading to their early Christmas party destinations.

As they pulled to the curb in front of Gaston's mansion, Ethan killed the engine and turned to her. "I love you, Jane."

She leaned across the console and kissed him. "I love you too."

Gaston met them on the porch, sipping blood from a coffee mug. "Good evening, friends. You're looking stunning as usual, Miss Jane."

She ran her hands down her dark red sweater. "Aw, thanks, Gaston. You're not so bad yourself. Have you had a look at Genevieve today?"

He smiled. "Indeed, I have. I'll have to send Santa my thanks."

Jane giggled. A three-hundred-year-old vampire writing a letter to Santa. How cute. "How's it going in there?"

He took another sip from his mug and nodded thoughtfully. "I must say, I see where you get your… outspokenness from."

"Daddy likes to talk, that's for sure. Y'all didn't tell him anything yet?"

He shook his head. "Sophie informed me of the cover story. You had an important business meeting that had to be conducted today, and that's why you were unable to pick him up from the airport."

"Good." His flight had gotten in at two in the afternoon, so she'd enlisted her BFF to entertain her dad until the sun set. Now, it was Jane's turn.

She nodded at his cup. "What's your poison?"

"Whiskey. Shall I make you one? I am the host with the most tonight."

"You got that right!" She took the glass from his hand and tossed back the contents. Hey, she needed a little liquid courage. "I'd love one. Thanks." She handed him the glass, opened the door, and stepped inside.

"Well, well. Look what the cat dragged in." Sophie

grinned and brushed her blonde hair behind her shoulders as she strode toward Jane and hugged her. She wore a cream tunic-length sweater with dark-brown leggings and boots. "It's about time you two got here."

"Hey, Soph. Thanks for holding down the fort."

"Any time." She hugged Ethan, and then Trace, her werewolf boyfriend, stepped forward and shook their hands. His dark brown eyes were nearly the same color as his hair and beard, and tiny lines formed around them as he smiled.

"Thanks for the invite," he said. "Merry Christmas."

"Thank Gaston for playing host." Jane peered over Trace's shoulder and glimpsed her dad standing by an armchair. He wore beige slacks and a crisp blue button-up, and she gave Ethan's hand a squeeze before padding toward him. "Hey, Daddy."

"Janey, sweetheart." He gave her one of his famous bear hugs, squeezing her so tight she might have popped if she wasn't a nearly-indestructible vampire. Then he held on. And on. Extending the hug into awkward territory.

"Whoa." She let out a nervous laugh. "I've missed you too."

He pulled back, resting his hands on her shoulders. "What was so important that you couldn't take the time to pick your old man up from the airport?"

"Work, Dad. I'm sorry I couldn't get away." She patted his hand and ducked out of his grasp. "I'm sure you of all people understand how that goes…seeing as how you're leaving Christmas morning so you can work that evening."

"It can't be called the Governor's Christmas Dinner if the Governor isn't in attendance." He chuckled, shaking his head. "The apples don't fall far from the tree, but I wasn't prepared to lose my youngest so quickly."

"You haven't lost me. I just live a little farther away now." She waved Ethan over, and he strode toward them with his back straight, doing a wonderful job at hiding his nerves. "Dad, this is my…" She almost said husband, but she caught herself before she let it slip. She needed to schmooze him a bit. Build up to the big reveal. "This is Ethan."

"Nice to meet you, sir." Ethan offered his hand, and her dad shook it.

"Merry Christmas." He cut his gaze between Ethan and Jane, arching a brow at her like he suspected they were an item, and why wouldn't he? Their chemistry had been off the charts since day one, even when Ethan thought he hated her.

Jane cleared her throat. "Let's sit and talk. Who wants eggnog?" She sent her thoughts to Gaston. *"You bought everything on the list, right?"*

"Yes, but I refuse to serve such an exquisite beverage from a plastic jug. I bought eggs and cream and made it myself… the old-fashioned way."

"Wow. I'm surprised you remembered how."

"It's a drink made with rum. How could I forget? I only wish the mixture would carry the liquor into my system the way blood does. I was rather fond of eggnog back in the time."

"Back in the day?"

"That's what I said." Gaston strode to the kitchen, and Jane joined the others in the living room.

"How's the dog-walking business going, Sophie?" Jane's father asked.

"Fantastic. I've got a waiting list a mile long, so I'll be hiring help soon. Between that and planning our wedding, I'm busy, busy, busy." She pressed her lips together, flashing an apologetic smile at Jane.

Talking about Sophie's wedding might lead her dad to ask about her own romantic situation, so Jane tucked her left hand under her thigh, hiding the ring her father hadn't noticed yet.

"New Orleans is a great place to live, though," Sophie continued, her voice taking on a nervous edge. "Right, Jane? You're doing great."

She forced a smile. "Never better. I love it here."

Ethan's hand curled into a fist on his leg. *"Can we get this over with, please?"*

"Yes, yes. Just give me a minute." Why was she having such a hard time telling her dad the truth? He would either take it in stride or blow his top. It was time they found out which. She opened her mouth to speak, but her dad cut her off.

"How long have you two been together?" He looked at Ethan and then at her.

Ethan took her hand. "Since February."

"February?" Her dad blinked. "That's a long time to keep your relationship a secret, isn't it?"

"I wasn't keeping it a secret. It just never came up." Her slowly beating heart picked up the pace, and she chewed her bottom lip. Now it was her turn to crack a chestnut between her cheeks. *Just spit it out, girl.* If only it were so easy…

Her dad rubbed his thumb and forefinger on his chin. "I suppose that's my fault. I should have come out to see you sooner." He chuckled. "I guess we've both been busy. So, how did you meet?"

"It's a funny story, actually." Jane gave Sophie a *help me out here* look, but all her BFF did was shrug and shake her head. Jane shot her the stink eye out of habit, but honestly, what could Sophie have done? This was Jane's story, and she had to be the one to tell it.

She squared her shoulders. "Ethan saved my life. That's how we met."

"Oh?" Her dad straightened, leaning forward. "How?"

Another nervous laugh bubbled from her chest. "I was taking some photos near the Lafayette Cemetery, and I kinda sorta stumbled into the street. A truck hit me, and then Ethan came to my rescue."

"Wha—?" He blew out a hard breath. He was getting worked up over nothing, but this was all part of Jane's plan. "Was the driver stopped? Were they arrested?"

"It was a hit and run."

"But you saw it." He locked his gaze on Ethan, who stiffened. "Surely you got the license plate."

Ethan started to answer, but Gaston sauntered in, carrying a tray of drinks. "Eggnog for the li…lovely guests." His eyes widened briefly as he glanced at Jane.

"You were going to say 'the living,' weren't you?" she thought-asked.

"My apologies. I assumed you'd told him by now."

"I'm working on it."

Gaston passed out the drinks, handing her and Ethan ceramic mugs of blood before returning to the kitchen. They both rested a hand on top of their cups, hiding the contents.

"The truck didn't stop," she continued her story, "and Ethan was focused on saving me. Without him, I wouldn't be here talking to you right now."

Her dad drummed his fingers on the arm of the chair. "Where were you when it happened? We can pull the video from the traffic cameras."

Ugh. He was focusing on the wrong part of the situation. "It's okay. I'm fine now, thanks to Ethan."

"It's most certainly not okay. Why didn't you tell me? We have to—"

"Dad," Jane raised her voice. "I'm okay. Shouldn't you be thanking Ethan for saving me rather than going off on a tangent about punishing someone we'll never find?"

His mouth opened and closed a few times like he wanted to press the issue, but he'd argued with Jane enough to recognize her tone. She was done talking about that part of the story, and thankfully, he gave in. "You're right. I owe you my gratitude, young man. Thank you for saving my daughter's life. I'm grateful she's alive to share this Christmas with us."

"Well…" Jane cringed. That was the perfect segue into what she needed to say, but good goat almighty, it didn't make it any easier. "I'm not sure 'alive' is the best word to describe my condition."

He stared at her, his eyes calculating, his mind most likely putting the pieces together while his stubbornness refused to let him accept it. He was going to make her say it, dammit.

She leaned forward and set her mug of blood on the coffee table, pausing and giving him time to see the contents. Then, Ethan set his cup next to hers.

Her dad swallowed hard, his expression a mix of confusion and terror as he looked at Sophie. She set her mug of eggnog on the table by the blood, and her dad blinked like he was doing Morse Code with his eyes.

Trace sipped his eggnog, oblivious to their silent conversation, until Sophie elbowed him in the ribs. "What?" He looked at the table and then at everyone staring at him. "Oh, sorry. I thought we were really supposed to drink these." He set his half-empty cup on the table. "Best eggnog I've ever had, Gaston," he called into the kitchen.

"Thank you. I can send you the recipe," Gaston replied.

Jane waited a moment or two for her dad to let it all sink in before she said, "I'm a vampire."

His gaze dropped to the table again, focusing on the two mugs of blood before he glared at her husband. "You!"

"I was going to die. He turned me to save me."

"No." Her dad shook his head. "No, you should have taken her to the hospital. You should have let the doctors save her."

"She wouldn't have made it to the hospital." Ethan wrapped his arm around her shoulders. "The truck ran her completely over like she was nothing more than a speed-bump. Her ribcage was crushed, both her lungs punctured. Turning her was the only way to save her."

"I don't believe that. An ambulance could have..."

"I had minutes," Jane said. "Less than minutes. If Ethan hadn't turned me when he did, I would not be sitting here right now."

"She is correct." Gaston finally decided to offer his assistance. "I was there when it happened. He would not have turned her if it weren't a dire emergency."

Her dad kept shaking his head like he couldn't accept it, his gaze bouncing around the room, looking at everything but Jane. Then, he leaned back on the couch and turned to Sophie. "And you knew?"

She nodded. "I let her drink from me to get her license."

"There's nothing you can do to change this, Dad, so

you'll have to accept it." Jane extended her fangs. "I'm a vampire, and I'm happier undead than I ever was alive."

Her dad took a deep breath, blowing it out hard and slumping his shoulders. He'd accepted her fate, but he didn't look thrilled about it. "You're a vampire," he said to Jane. "And you turned her." He pointed at Ethan. "And you…?" He looked at Gaston, who sat on the arm of the sofa next to Jane.

"I'm Ethan's sire. I turned him twenty-five years ago, and I can vouch for him. He's a good man, like Jane is a good woman. They belong together."

"Aw. That's the nicest thing you've ever said about me, old man," she said. No, those weren't tears gathering in her eyes. It was allergies. Leftover fairy dust. *Something*.

Her dad nodded and looked at Sophie again. "You two are human?"

Sophie glanced at Trace. "Not anymore," she said.

"Anymore?" He arched a brow.

"Soph, you never were," Jane said. If she was being honest with her dad, her bestie would have to as well.

"Okay," Sophie said. "I was born a witch, but I didn't know it because my grandma died when my dad was young. Trace is a werewolf."

"And…?" Jane tapped her foot.

Sophie stuck out her tongue. "I'm a werewolf too. Trace accidentally bit me a few months ago, but that's a story for another day."

Her dad sighed, giving Jane his signature look of disappointment. She'd grown so used to seeing the expression over the years, she accepted it as his normal face now. Closing his eyes, he inhaled deeply, letting his breath out slowly. Then, he did it again, really laying on the drama. After his fourth deep breath, her dad looked at her. "Why didn't you tell me about this when it happened? I could have helped you." He spoke to her just like he did when she was five years old and had broken her mother's antique vase.

"Helped me how? By dragging me back to Texas and locking me in my bedroom for the rest of eternity?"

"Jane, honey, I wouldn't have locked you in your room." The condescending tone of his voice ripped open the old wound. The man never did believe she was capable of taking care of herself.

"No? In the basement, then? I didn't need your help, Dad, just like I didn't need you to send a babysitter when Sophie and I were here for Mardi Gras." She shot to her feet and paced in front of the couch. Who was dramatic now?

"Yes, I had an accident," she continued, "but it was exactly that. An accident. It could have happened to anyone, and I didn't tell you about it because I knew you would overreact, just like you do about everything when it comes to me."

"Jane, calm down." He stood and reached for her arm, but she jerked away.

"No, let me finish. I waited until now to tell you because I wanted you to see how responsible I am. I have a good job. I've settled down; I'm living in one place, and I'm *happy*." She stopped pacing and faced him. "I'm not the helpless little girl you keep insisting I am. Open your eyes, Dad. I'm a grown woman."

"Jane is absolutely killing it as a vampire," Sophie said. "I mean...she's not *literally* killing anything. She runs the hottest undead nightclub in New Orleans, and she's good friends with the Magistrate. She gets shit done. You should be proud of her."

Jane mouthed the words *thank you* to her bestie for coming to her defense.

"You told me your club hadn't opened yet," her dad said.

"If I couldn't tell you I was a vampire, I sure as hell couldn't tell you I was running a vampire blood bar. It's called Nocturnal New Orleans, and it's been open for a few months now."

"But I researched every bar in this state."

She expected nothing less from her father, and that was precisely the reason she told him so little about the concept…because he'd check up on her like always.

"None of them listed Jane Anderson as the owner," he said. "Not even that one."

"That's because my name isn't Anderson anymore. She took Ethan's hand, holding it in both of hers. "It's Devereaux. Ethan and I married."

He gasped like he'd just received the most shocking news of his life. "You got married and didn't invite your own father to the wedding?" He seemed more upset about her relationship status than the fact she was undead.

"We didn't have a wedding, so there was nothing to invite you to. The Magistrate married us. Sophie and Gaston were the witnesses, and no one else was there." She shrugged. "We just wanted to be married. We didn't need all the pomp and circumstance."

"I see." His eyes narrowed, and he gave his head a tiny shake like he always did when he didn't approve of her choices. With a huff, he turned on his heel and marched up the stairs.

She'd done it now. The man who always had to have the last word had nothing to say to her. *Fan-friggin-tastic.* Ethan started toward the stairs, but she caught him by the arm and shook her head. "Best to let him cool off first."

A few minutes later, her dad came down carrying his suitcase and stomped toward the front door. "This is too much. I can't discuss this right now."

"Where are you going?" she asked.

He paused with his hand on the doorknob. "To a hotel. A taxi is on its way." Without so much as a good-bye, he slipped out the door, pulling it shut behind him.

"That went well." Trace picked up his eggnog and took another sip.

Jane groaned. "He's so dramatic."

"Like father, like daughter." Gaston grinned.

"Bite me."

"I prefer the living, thank you."

"Shouldn't we go after him?" Ethan touched her elbow, gently steering her toward the door.

"If he wants time, give it to him." Jane took a long gulp from her mug, closing her eyes as the whiskey-laced blood warmed her icy throat. "He's not mad. He's disappointed."

"Ouch," Sophie said.

"Tell me about it." Jane finished the rest of her drink.

"What is he disappointed about? That you're a vampire?" Ethan asked.

She shrugged. "Maybe. Or that I got married without his blessing. Or maybe that I got run over at all. He'll probably come back tomorrow and lecture me about looking both ways before I cross the street."

Sophie laughed. "Remember that time Susan Wilks got caught shoplifting in high school? He lectured us both for a full hour on why we shouldn't steal, and we weren't even with her when it happened!"

"He loves the sound of his own voice. And being right." She plopped onto the couch.

Ethan sank down next to her. "You're really not going to go after him? He came all this way."

"What am I supposed to do? Chase him down and beg him to love me? Jane Devereaux does not grovel. You know that."

"I'm so sorry, hun." Sophie sat on the loveseat. "I thought he'd take it better than that."

"You weren't there for my goth phase in junior high. He wouldn't be seen with me in public because I didn't fit his ideal of the perfect child." And now he had a vampire for a daughter. Why in Hades did she think he'd take it in stride?

"Maybe we should go." Trace rested a hand on Sophie's shoulder. "Give them some space."

"But I bought all this food," Gaston pleaded. "And I got games."

"And we're going to enjoy them," Jane said. "How about another round of drinks, Gaston? I'll get the board game set up."

Ethan took her hand as she stood. "Are you sure?"

"I'm not going to let my father ruin our Christmas."

CHAPTER EIGHT

The phone buzzing on the nightstand roused Jane from the death sleep, and she squinted at the clock. 6:30 P.M. That had to be the earliest she'd awoken since the day she died. Of course, Ethan had been up since sunset, as usual, and she found herself alone in the king-sized bed.

She and her friends had played a few games and had a couple of drinks before everyone turned in early. Not exactly the party she had planned, but tonight would be better…with or without her dad.

Swinging her legs to the floor, she gripped the phone and pressed it to her ear. "Hello?" Her throat was dry and scratchy, but she forgot all about her thirst when the reply came through.

"Hi, Jane. It's Cindy Claus."

Hell's bells. She could only think of one reason why the queen of the fae would be calling on Christmas Eve. "Is Santa… Did he…?"

"Santa is fine. He's out delivering gifts as we speak."

Her breath of relief came out in a whoosh. "Thank the devil. I was worried there for a hot minute."

Cindy's laugh reminded her of jingle bells. "He asked me to call and let you know your father is staying at the Hotel Monteleone. If you hurry, you may be able to catch him and make both your Christmas wishes come true."

She cradled the phone between her shoulder and her ear as she pulled on her pants. "What's his wish? To see me beg for forgiveness?"

"I'm not at liberty to discuss another person's wish, but I can assure you that's not it. Your father loves you."

Jane sighed. She knew that much; she only wished he'd stop looking at her like she was ten years old. "How does Santa know he's staying there? I thought he didn't mess with humans anymore."

"Santa knows where everyone is."

She nodded, though Cindy couldn't see her response. "I suppose he does." And she supposed she should try to make up with her father. Jane may have had all the time in the world, but her dad wouldn't be around forever. Just because he treated her like a child, it didn't mean she had to act like one.

"Thanks, Cindy. I appreciate the tip."

"You're very welcome. Merry Christmas."

After Jane hung up the phone, she finished getting dressed and ran downstairs for a quick drink. Gaston and Ethan sat on the couch watching *National Lampoon's Christmas Vacation* on the flat screen mounted above the fireplace, and Gaston chuckled as the poor Griswolds tried to catch the crazy squirrel running loose in their house.

She chugged a glass of blood to soothe the desert in her throat and then kissed Ethan on the cheek. "I'm going to talk to my dad."

He caught her hand before she could walk away. "I'll come with you."

"No." She gave his hand a squeeze and let it go. "Let me talk to him alone. It may be the only way to get through to him." In hindsight, she should have had the conversation one-on-one to begin with. Jane had wanted her friends there for moral support, but her dad had probably felt threatened by the pack. Duh, she was friends with werewolves. She should have known the dynamic would offend an alpha male like her father.

Ethan nodded and handed her his car keys. "Be careful out there."

Gaston's gaze remained glued to the screen. "Try not to run anyone else over."

"Funny."

As she stepped onto the porch, a gust of cold wind blew her hair into her face. She tucked it behind her ears and trekked to the car parked on the curb. Thankfully, traffic was minimal on Christmas Eve, and she made it to the French Quarter quickly. Her dad had just stepped out the front doors of Hotel Monteleone when she pulled up and rolled down the window.

"Get in the car, Dad. We need to talk."

Her father paused, looking to the right and then the left, almost as if searching for an escape path. Apparently, he couldn't find an easy way out because he frowned and made his way toward the car.

Resting a hand on the top of the Taurus, he leaned into the window. "I can't talk now. I'm on my way to an appointment."

"I'll drive you."

He sighed and climbed into the passenger seat.

"Where are you going?"

He cleared his throat as he fastened his seatbelt. "I have a meeting with your Magistrate."

Jane's eyes widened, her mouth falling open as she processed his words. "The Magistrate? Why? What are you going to do?" Her pitch took on a nervous edge. Being upset with her was one thing, but if he made this political…

"Relax, Janey." He finally looked at her. "I just want the official, unbiased account of what happened to you."

"That better be it." She clutched the steering wheel in a death grip. "I won't let you start shit here. This is *my* life you're messing with."

A car horn blared behind her, and a valet knocked on her window. "Hey, Miss. You have to move."

"Yeah, yeah." Jane waved a hand dismissively.

Her dad reached for the door handle. "Either you drive me to your coven house, or I will take a cab."

Jane growled low in her throat and put the car in drive. "Fine. But I'm coming inside with you."

They were silent on the short drive through the French Quarter, and by the time she parked in front of the coven's nineteenth-century mansion, her jaw ached from gnashing her teeth. She got out of the car, slamming the door and using her vampire speed to shoot up the sidewalk before her dad could even get his seatbelt off.

She crossed her arms as he climbed out of the car and looked at her. He opened his mouth as if to speak, but he just shook his head and strolled toward her, gesturing for her to go up the walk first.

"I'm surprised the Magistrate agreed to see you on Christmas Eve." She opened the front door and stepped inside, waiting for her dad to follow.

"He took no issue with my request once he found out

who I am." He walked into the sitting room and clasped his hands behind his back as he gazed into an antique mirror.

"I bet." Jane started toward the entrance that would lead to the Council's chambers, but the door swung open, and old Willy himself greeted them.

"Jane." The Magistrate nodded at her before focusing on her dad. "Mr. Anderson, it's a pleasure to meet you. Won't you come back?"

"Thank you." Her dad walked through the door, but Willy put a hand up when Jane tried to follow.

"Wait here."

"But—"

He had the nerve to close the door right in her face! "Typical," she grumbled and plopped onto the chaise lounge near the piano. Reaching across the arm, she tapped a white key, and a melodic C rang out from the instrument. She could only imagine the stories Willy must've been telling her dad.

Her phone vibrated, and she tugged it from her pocket to find a text from Ethan: *How's it going?*

She typed her reply: *Don't ask. He's meeting with the Magistrate right now.*

Ethan's response was three question marks, followed by: *We're on our way.*

"Ugh. No. That's the last thing I need." She hit the call button, and he answered immediately.

"I'm climbing into Genevieve now. Hang tight."

"It's fine, Ethan. Y'all don't have to come here. Just stay put."

The car door slammed. "Gaston and I will take care of you, Jane. Whatever he's trying to do, we won't let it happen."

"I appreciate your chivalry, my love; I really do. But he's not trying to *do* anything. He just wants to read the official account of what happened to me."

"Are you sure? We can be there in ten minutes if you need us."

"I'm sure. My relationship with my father might be in danger, but my life is not. Neither is yours." She rose to her feet and paced across the plush rug. "He's still coming to terms with everything. Give me a little more time with him, okay?"

"Okay, but promise me you'll call if anything happens."

"What do you think he's going to do? Have his own daughter staked? It'll be fine. I'll meet you at Gaston's in an hour or two. Dad might be with me, and he might not." She shrugged. That was what it all boiled down to: he'd either accept her new life and be a part of it, or he wouldn't.

She hung up the phone and waited. And waited. And waited. When her dad finally returned to the sitting room, his expression was unreadable.

"We should go," he said. "The Magistrate said to tell you he'll see you in the new year."

Yeah, she could read between the lines on that one. Willy meant he better not *have* to see her before then, or there would be hell to pay. *I'll try my best.*

They got into the car, and she started the engine, but she didn't drive. "Can we talk about this now?"

Her dad buckled his seatbelt. "Why were we staying at Gaston's house and not your own?"

Not exactly the conversation she wanted to have at the moment, but at least the man was talking. "Because our house is small. We wanted Sophie and Trace to be there for the holiday too, and I thought you'd be more comfortable in a mansion."

"Why is your house small?" He stared straight ahead.

"Because it is." She drew her shoulders toward her ears. Where was he going with this?

"Have you spent all of your trust? Can you not afford a suitable place to live?"

Ah, there it was. Back to the *Jane can't take care of herself* mindset. "Our house is more than suitable. It's very nice, and I've hardly spent any of my trust since I died. My job pays really well. Ethan's too."

He shook his head. "Don't say that. Don't say you died."

"But I did. I died, and thanks to Ethan, I came back as a vampire. I'm not alive anymore, Dad. I'm undead."

Closing his eyes, he blew out a long, slow breath. "Will you show me where you live...or...stay?"

"Yeah, of course." She put the car in drive and headed to Marigny, just outside the French Quarter. A crowd had gathered on Frenchman Street to watch a five-piece brass band perform Christmas tunes, and she slowed to a crawl to avoid running over any tourists. See, she learned from her mistakes.

"Ethan lived here for around thirty years before I met him." She parked on the curb in front of their home.

Her dad looked out the window at the small Creole-style cottage with brown paint and blue shutters. "It's quaint."

"It's a great place to live. We have two bedrooms and a nice size living room. We aren't too far from the coven house, and the French Quarter is just a few blocks away, so there's plenty of..."

"Plenty of what?" He arched a brow.

"Well, it's no secret what we eat." She sighed. "Do you want to see the inside?"

"I want to see where it happened."

"Where what happened?" She swallowed hard. "The accident?"

"Where you…died."

Why on earth would he want to put himself through that? Even she didn't care to remember being a speedbump for a pickup truck. "Daddy, I don't think—"

"Please, Jane. I need to see where it happened."

"Alrighty then. But there's really nothing to see now. The bloodstains have been washed away."

He sucked in a sharp breath, and Jane bit her tongue. It was probably best if she held it for the rest of the drive to the Garden District. She'd only been dead ten months, but she was already forgetting what it was like to be human sometimes.

She parked under a massive oak tree in front of Lafayette Cemetery #1 and waited on the sidewalk for her dad. He shoved his hands in his pockets and slowly walked toward her, his gaze bouncing around the area as he took in the scene.

Black iron gates closed the entrance to the cemetery, and rows of above-ground tombs stretched back to the end of the block. Some were well-kept, with flowers adorning vases in front of the graves, while others appeared weathered, the white stucco façades giving way to the brick and mortar beneath. Across the way, two-story, white wooden houses lined the street.

"This is it?" His breath came out as a fog in the cold night air, and an owl hooted from inside the cemetery.

When he stopped beside her, she gestured to the road. "Right there. I was trying to get a good picture." She motioned to the brick wall behind her. "I didn't hear the truck over the parade noises a block that way."

Clouds covered the moon, making the area appear darker than she remembered, more deserted. Why the hell wasn't she scared that night? A normal human would have been, but Jane had never been accused of being normal.

Her dad looked up and down the street. "And he... turned you...right here in the road?"

"Oh, no. That would have been dangerous. He scooped me up and took me into the cemetery before he bit me."

"Show me where he took you."

"Umm..." Why was he doing this to himself? "The gates are locked, so..."

"How did he get you inside?"

"He jumped."

"Jumped?"

"Over the wall." She pointed to the seven-feet-high wall separating the graves from the sidewalk. "Vampires are super-strong."

"Show me."

She blinked, hesitating. "Show you? As in you want me to pick you up and jump over the wall with you?"

"Precisely."

Seriously? Had her dad smoked something before he got in the car tonight? "Why? What happened happened, and it can't be changed. It doesn't matter if he turned me in a cemetery or in a bathtub at the Ritz. I'm a vampire."

"And if I'm going to accept that fact, I need to see where it happened."

Jeez Louise. The man couldn't take no for an answer. "Fine." She wrapped her arms around his waist. "I've never tried this before, so it might be awkward, but…here we go."

With a spring of her knees, she vaulted onto the top of the wall and set her dad on the stone. "I was afraid to go all the way over without seeing what we'd be landing on."

His eyes were wide with wonder as he looked at her and tilted his head like he didn't believe what just happened. What, did he think she was making it all up? "This is fine. I can climb down from here." He sat on the wall and lowered himself to the ground.

Jane turned toward the road to be sure no one had seen her little stunt, but as she spun back around, her stiletto got caught in a crack, and she stumbled. With a squeal, she fell head over heels, skewering herself on a decorative wrought-iron post next to a tomb.

The pointed edge pierced her cashmere sweater, going straight through her back and coming out her stomach on the other side. *Ouch.* "Damn it. This was my favorite outfit."

"Jane! Oh, honey, no!" Her dad rushed to her side.

"I'm fine. Just let me…" She reached behind her back to grab the pole and yanked it from the ground as she righted herself. Looking down at her ruined clothes, she raked her hands through her hair. "Just my luck."

Her dad was as white as a corpse in a snowstorm. "You're okay? You're not even bleeding!"

"Yeah. Vampires don't really bleed. Can you give me a hand?" She gripped the post. If it had pierced her a few inches higher she'd have been toast. *Yikes.* "Grab it here and pull."

"Maybe we should take you to the hospital." He looked like he was about to hurl, his pallor turning from white to green.

"Vampires definitely don't go to hospitals. It didn't hit my heart, so I'll be fine. Just pull."

He nodded, swallowed hard, and yanked the pole from her gut.

"Son of a bitch!" It felt like…well, it felt like someone stabbed her through with an iron pole and then yanked it out. There was no other way to describe it. She lifted her shirt to examine the wound, and a single drop of red trailed toward her belly button. "Oh, look. I'm bleeding a little. Sweet!" She wiped the blood from her stomach and brought it to her lips.

Her dad looked at the post in his hand and then at her, his mouth opening and closing like he wanted to say something, but his brain wouldn't let him. His eyes were wide and unblinking, and the green tint hadn't quite left his complexion.

"I'm fine, see?" She gestured to the wound. "It's already healing. You won't even know it happened five minutes from now. Being undead isn't all bad, you know."

He shook his head. "You used to faint at the sight of blood. How did you overcome that?"

"I didn't have a choice, did I? You'd be surprised at what I can accomplish when no one is hovering over me, waiting for me to fall so they can catch me."

He held up the skewer.

She laughed. "Okay, that time would have been nice if you'd caught me, but other than that…"

The shock finally faded from his expression, a look of sincerity taking its place. "You are a very capable young woman, Jane. I've always known that." He tossed the post aside and placed a hand on her shoulder. "I'm sorry I made you feel otherwise."

"Thank you for saying that." Actions spoke louder than words, but it was a start. She'd take it.

"So this is where it happened?"

"Yep." She strolled toward the spot where Ethan had turned her. Truth be told, she didn't remember much about the ordeal, but he'd brought her back here and showed her the place on their six-month anniversary. "He turned me here, and then he took me home, and we are living happily ever after."

"Do you love him?"

"Of course I do. I wouldn't have married him if I didn't."

"I mean, are you sure it's really love and not a spell? You're positive you aren't just fond of him because he's your sire?"

"First, vampires can't cast spells. Well, maybe if they were a witch before they were turned, but a normal vampire can't. Our glamour only allows us to put people into a trance, make them forget things, or make them see things that aren't there. Ethan couldn't deceive me into loving him if he tried." She sat on a stone bench next to an above-ground tomb. "And if every vampire fell in love with their sire, that would make for some awkward relationships. I love Ethan because he's a wonderful man and a perfect partner."

He sat down next to her. "Your Magistrate says you're an asset to the organization here. He had nothing but good things to say about you."

That was a shocker, but if Willy didn't feel the need to tell him how many times he'd wanted to stake her, she'd keep her mouth shut. "I'm learning everything I can about vampire politics. Once I'm eligible, I plan to run for a seat on the Council."

"Really?" His lips twitched before tugging upward into a smile. "You want to get into politics?"

"Hell yeah, I do. If anyone can make a difference in Louisiana's supernatural government, it's a governor's daughter."

He nodded and took her hand. "You truly are happy here, aren't you?"

"I love my undead life."

"But you'll have to watch your family grow old and die."

She shrugged. She'd come to terms with all of this months ago. "I'm the youngest. That was going to happen anyway."

His eyes softened. "You'll never have children."

"I never wanted them." Siring Santa was confirmation of that. "And you've got four other kids. You'll be drowning in grandbabies any day now."

"I suppose that's true. So, I guess there's only one thing left to do." He tugged his wallet from his pocket and pulled out a small velvet bag from inside. "You might recognize this. It was your mother's."

As she held out her hand, he placed a gold bracelet in her palm. Six bezel-set rubies were evenly spaced along the delicate chain, and her breath caught at the sight of it. "She never took it off."

"I gave it to her on our wedding day, and before she died, she asked me to give it to you on your wedding day. I've been carrying it around ever since."

Jane's lower lip trembled as she realized how hurt her dad must have been to learn she'd gotten married without including him. He'd been waiting for the day to fulfill her mom's dying wish, and she'd taken it away from him. Yep, she was definitely a big ole bitch. "Oh, Dad. I'm so sorry."

"Nonsense, sweetheart. You have to live your life the way you see fit." He took the bracelet and clasped it around her wrist. "You're a grown woman, and you don't need our blessing, but you have it. Your mother's and mine."

She threw her arms around his neck, the weight of her secrets lifting—now that they were finally revealed—and coming out as a sob. Sure, she may have said it was no big deal if he couldn't accept her, but deep down, it was her greatest wish. "I love you, Dad."

"I love you too, Jane." He held her for a moment or two while she got her blubbering under control before he said, "Is there anything else you need to tell me? Any more life-altering shenanigans you've gotten yourself into?"

"That about covers it." She'd spare him the details of her run-in—err…run-over—with Santa. Her dad had endured enough.

He pulled away, clutching her shoulders and gazing into her eyes. "If I'm still invited, I'd love to spend Christmas Eve with my daughter and her husband."

She wiped a tear from her cheek. "Of course you're still invited. You're welcome anytime."

She carried him over the wall, and they made the short drive to the Garden District mansion. When they entered the house, he shook Gaston's hand. "I'd like to apologize for my behavior. That was no way for a grown man to act, and I do appreciate your hospitality."

"We've been around Jane for nearly a year now," Gaston said, and he winked at her. "It's nothing we haven't seen before."

She made a face at him as her dad turned to Ethan and shook his hand. "Do you love my daughter?" he asked.

"With every fiber of being."

He patted him on the shoulder. "Welcome to the family, son."

Ethan smiled. "Thank you, sir."

Her dad wrapped one arm around Ethan's shoulders and the other around hers, pulling them tight to his sides. "Well, I've gained a son-in-law, and my daughter wants to go into politics. I suppose I couldn't ask for a better Christmas."

"Neither could I." Jingling bells sounded from outside, and a faint *ho, ho, ho* drifted on the air, making Jane smile. So much for Santa not being able to grant her Christmas wish.

"If I have my house equipped with your fancy vampire shutters, will you and Ethan come and visit?"

"We'd love to," Ethan said.

"I'd like to give you a party. I know you didn't want to make a big deal out of your wedding, but your marriage… and your undead lives…are something to celebrate. Plus, the Governor's daughter can't get married without a little pomp and circumstance."

"Daddy…"

"Just a small reception with a few hundred of our closest friends. Humor me?"

Jane toyed with the bracelet on her wrist and laughed. "Well, I do love throwing parties."

CHAPTER NINE

Fingertips caressed Jane's forehead, running through her hair as she lay nestled in the sheets of the king-sized bed in one of Gaston's many guest rooms. A thick blue comforter lay across her, not because vampires got cold when they slept, but because it was the coziest feeling in the world, lying there with her husband, cuddling beneath the weight of the blanket.

When she opened her eyes, she found Ethan gazing at her, his green eyes glistening in the soft moonlight that streamed in through the window.

He smiled and pressed a kiss to her lips. "Good evening, princess."

"Come here, you." She snuggled against his side, tossing her leg across his hips and nuzzling into his neck. "We survived Christmas Eve."

He traced his fingers along her bare arm, raising goose-bumps on her skin. "It wasn't nearly as bad as I thought it would be."

They'd made it through the bomb-drop on her dad with no casualties and then spent the rest of the night talking and laughing, catching up on each other's lives. The living had finally turned in around two a.m., and the vampires followed near dawn.

Sophie had taken her dad to the airport in the morning, and Jane was actually looking forward to the party he wanted to throw for her and her husband.

Ethan wrapped his arms around her, holding her tighter, his voice taking on a deep, sexy rumble as he spoke. "Gaston has plenty of blood in the fridge. How about I grab us each a bottle, and we spend the rest of the night in bed?"

"I like the way you think." It had been days since Vlad had come out to play, and she couldn't wait to be impaled, but… "There's something we need to do first."

"Mmm. Let's do it second. Gaston was such a good host, I almost feel like we're in a hotel. And hotel sex is mind-blowing."

Jane laughed and rolled out of bed to pull on her jeans. "Any sex with you is mind-blowing. Come on. Get up. It's time for your Christmas present."

He pursed his lips, not moving from the bed. "I thought we agreed to no gifts. We already have everything we could ever want."

"I know, but I couldn't help myself." She tossed him his shirt. "Hurry. They might leave if we're late."

"They?" He slid out of bed and got dressed. "Who's they?"

"Uh-uh. I'm not ruining the surprise. Let's go." She practically pranced down the hall toward the staircase, excitement bubbling in her chest as she made her way downstairs. At least, she thought the sensation was excitement.

She paused at the bottom of the steps and tapped her

fist against her chest to see if she needed to burp. Nope, it was definitely excitement.

Gaston sat in the living room, reading a newspaper. Jane had tried to show him how easy it was to use the news app on his phone, but the ancient vampire preferred to read the old-fashioned way.

"Good evening, Gaston." She kissed him on the cheek before heading for the door.

"Hello, Miss Jane."

"Thanks again, man." Ethan stopped in front of him and shook his hand. "For everything."

"It was my pleasure. I rather enjoyed playing host last night. So much so that I'm considering renting out my rooms as a supernatural bed and breakfast."

"That's a fantastic idea." Jane gripped the doorknob and bounced on her toes.

"It's time I found a new purpose in my existence. Perhaps this will be it."

"Let me know if you need any help setting things up." Jane waved Ethan over. "C'mon, c'mon, c'mon. Let's goooooo…"

"There is never a dull moment with Jane Devereaux around, is there?" Gaston asked.

"No. No, there is not." Ethan laughed and followed her onto the porch.

"Eek! They're here! Look!" She pointed to the pair of jet-black Harley Davidsons sitting in the driveway. One bike had *Blitzen* scrawled across the gas tank, while the other read *Prancer*.

She darted down the steps toward the reindeer, and Ethan followed, pausing a few feet away.

"You got us motorcycles?" Confusion furrowed his brow.

Jane ran her hand over Blitzen's "seat," the contact allowing her to see through the magic. "Good job on the glamour, boys." She smiled at her husband. "Come touch him."

"Him?" Ethan stepped toward Prancer and touched the handlebar. "Satan's balls. They're reindeer! How?"

"Cindy. Don't get too excited, though. We only have them for the night." She climbed onto Blitzen's back and stroked the soft fur on his neck. "Ready to go for a ride?"

"Hell yeah, I am!" Ethan grinned like a kid on Christmas, which he kinda was at the moment…a big kid. "He's a lot taller than he looks. How do you get on? I don't want to spook him."

"Just like riding a horse bareback."

He shook his head, looking at her expectantly.

"Don't tell me you've never ridden a horse."

"Only when I was little, and then my mom put me on its back."

She laughed. "Okay. Put your left arm across the back of his neck. Use it as leverage when you jump and swing your leg over."

"Got it." He hopped onto Prancer's back like he'd done it a thousand times before.

"Damn. I was looking forward to watching you fall on your ass." Jane winked.

"I jumped over the cemetery wall with your dead weight in my arms. I think I can mount a deer."

She giggled. "You said 'mount.'"

"Oh, I'll be mounting you later, *cher*. Don't you worry."

"I can't wait." She tapped her heels against Blitzen's sides. "Race you to Audubon Park."

"You're on."

They rode through the Garden District toward the park, past grand Colonial and Victorian homes adorned with enough tinsel and holly to rival the North Pole. No wonder Santa liked coming here…New Orleans was a holiday wonderland—minus the snow, of course. It rarely snowed this close to the coast.

As they stopped at a light, Jane admired a white mansion with red garland spiraling up the Greek Revival columns, a wreath in every window, and twinkling lights hanging from every eave. But all that sparkle and jolly couldn't hold a candle to the way her husband's face lit up as he smiled.

"They can fly, can't they?" he asked.

Jane flashed a mischievous grin. "There's only one way to find out."

Heading down Magazine Street, they entered Audubon Park and rode around the walking trail encircling the golf course. The reindeer must have been mind-readers because they toned down the glamour volume, silencing the imaginary roar of engines as they loped deeper into the park, away from the road.

"I don't see any people around," Ethan said, "but we better activate our glamour too, just to be safe."

"On it." Jane used her magic to create a faux invisibility spell. Vampires didn't actually turn transparent when they used this type of glamour. Instead, their magic affected the minds of anyone who might look at them, making them instantly forget what they saw.

With Ethan's glamour activated, he patted Prancer's side. "Okay, boys. Let's fly."

At his command, the reindeer took to the sky, soaring above the trees and encircling the city. Cool wind blew through Jane's hair, and she squealed as she wrapped her arms around Blitzen's neck, once again holding on for *deer* life.

"Woo!" Ethan hooped and hollered loud enough to wake the dead...though most of them were probably already up. "This is amazing!"

They flew for another hour, the deer actually moving their legs through the air like they were running...just like in the movies...and Jane fought the urge to sing "I Can Show You the World" at the top of her lungs.

Well, she fought it for a little while, anyway. Then, she belted out the whole song as they took in the sights of the city from above.

Finally, Ethan led the way back home, and they landed on the curb in front of their house. "Thank you, Jane." He slid off the deer/Harley and offered her a hand down. "That was a dream come true."

"You're very welcome." She stepped into his arms and kissed him. His lips were soft, his body hard, and her mind drifted back to their very first kiss and the way his fangs extended and his dick hardened at her touch...just like now.

It was time for Vlad to come out and play.

"Thanks, boys," she said to the reindeer. "Give Cindy my best." She patted Blitzen on the flank, and they took to the sky, their silhouettes against the moon making the moment complete.

Ethan grasped her hand and led her inside to the bedroom. "Just when I think I've seen everything you can do, you bring Santa's reindeer home for a ride." He grabbed her ass and pulled her close, nipping at her neck. "You never cease to amaze me, princess."

"There are plenty more wonders to behold." She

tugged his shirt over his head and ran her fingers down his abs to unbutton his jeans. "Glorious wonders."

A masculine grunt emanated from his throat as he tore her sweater over her head and crushed his mouth to hers. Sweet baby Hades, he was like a starving predator going after his prey.

He pinned her back against the wall—which didn't hurt, thanks to her own vampire strength—and yanked her pants down. She stumbled a little as she worked her feet from the garment, but the moment she was free, she turned the tables, slamming him against the wall and jerking the rest of his clothes off.

He grinned wickedly as she unhooked her bra and then shimmied out of her panties. He licked his lips before touching the tip of his tongue to his fang. "You know that urge to rip each other's clothes off every time we touch?"

"Boy, do I."

"It gets stronger every day."

"I'm glad we can give in to it now."

"You and me both, *cher*." He took her in his arms, spinning her around and pinning her against the wall once more.

He glided his tongue between her breasts and down her stomach as he dropped to his knees. Leaning her head back, she spread her legs, giving her husband and his magic mouth access to her sweet spot.

As he bathed her sensitive nub with a cool swipe of his tongue, electricity shot through her core, making her entire body tingle. He gripped her hips and licked her some more, moaning right along with her as he pushed her closer and closer to the edge.

She cried out as the first orgasm consumed her—there were always multiple when it came to Ethan—and she clutched his shoulders, digging her nails into his skin as she rode the wave of ecstasy to the shore.

His pupils dilated as he rose to his feet, the desire in his eyes hot enough to melt skin from bone. After lifting her by the waist, he slid his hands down her legs, wrapping one around one hip and then the other.

With her back pressed against the wall, he filled her, a pleasurable ache spreading out to her thighs as he pulled out and filled her again. She gripped the back of his neck, kissing him like she was dying of thirst and he was the last drop of blood on earth.

His thrusts quickened, and another orgasm coiled in her core, releasing in an explosion in time with his, making lights twinkle in her peripheral vision like the grandest holiday display she'd ever seen.

He leaned into her, showering her in kisses before carrying her to the bed, and she lay against his side, wrapped in his arms and basking in their love. Never in her life had she felt safer or happier than she did with this man. Getting run over at Mardi Gras truly was the best thing that ever happened to her.

"I got you something." He smiled and reached for the nightstand drawer, pulling out a rectangular black box.

"I thought we agreed to no gifts." She bit her bottom lip.

"You reneged on the deal. So can I." He handed her the box.

"That's fair." She opened it, and her breath caught. Nestled in the black velvet interior lay a white gold necklace, the pendant shaped like an infinity symbol with two diamonds mounted in the center where it overlapped.

"It's beautiful. Will you put it on me?" She sat up and

turned her back to him, allowing him to drape the chain around her neck and fasten it. "I'll never take it off."

He wrapped his arms around her from behind and kissed her cheek. "When I saw it, I couldn't pass it up. Diamonds are forever, right?"

She leaned her head back on his shoulder, and he held her tighter. "Like vampires," she said.

"Like my love for you," he whispered into her ear.

ALSO BY CARRIE PULKINEN

Spirit Chasers Series

To Catch a Spirit

To Stop a Shadow

To Free a Phantom

Stand Alone Books

The Rest of Forever

Bewitching the Vampire

Soul Catchers

ABOUT THE AUTHOR

Carrie Pulkinen is a paranormal romance author who has always been fascinated with things that go bump in the night. Of course, when you grow up next door to a cemetery, the dead (and the undead) are hard to ignore. Pair that with her passion for writing and her love of a good happily-ever-after, and becoming a paranormal romance author seems like the only logical career choice.

Before she decided to turn her love of the written word into a career, Carrie spent the first part of her professional life as a high school journalism and yearbook teacher. She loves good chocolate and bad puns, and in her free time, she likes to read, drink wine, and travel with her family.

Connect with Carrie online:
www.CarriePulkinen.com

Made in the USA
Las Vegas, NV
10 March 2021